SHABBY STREET

A NOVEL BY

ORRIE
HITT

BLACKBIRD BOOKS
NEW YORK • LOS ANGELES

A Blackbird Classic, February 2012

Cover painting by Walter Popp

Manufactured in the United States of America.

The events and characters depicted in this book are fictional.

Cataloging-in-Publication Data

Hitt, Orrie.
Shabby street / Orrie Hitt.
p. cm.
1. Fraud—Fiction. 2. Embezzlement—Fiction. 3. Insurance—
Fiction. 4. New York (State)—Fiction. I. Title.
PS3558.I87 S53 2012 813'.54—dc22 2012931252

Blackbird Books
www.bbirdbooks.com
email us at editor@bbirdbooks.com

ISBN 978-1-61053-007-1

First Blackbird Edition

10 9 8 7 6 5 4 3 2 1

SHABBY STREET

CHAPTER I

Dark Passion

I SAT on my stool behind the hotel desk, thinking about the redhead who had just checked into two-four. Then I forgot all about her as the telephone girl started straightening her sweater in some interesting places.

"Lord!" Janet Hobbs sighed. "Only ten-thirty! Isn't this night ever going to end? Half-hour to go."

By my watch every night in this creep joint was too long. The rugs in the lobby were faded and the seats of the chairs sagged worse than the knees of my pants. The manager had a lousy disposition and a couple of ulcers as big as watermelons. One of the bellhops was always chasing strange-acting guys. After almost a month in the racket I was ready to get out of the hotel business for good.

I kept looking at Janet as she went about making her connections at the switchboard. There was one connection I was willing to bet she hadn't made yet. I'd only known her three weeks, but already I'd been thrown out near home a couple of times. That didn't bother me any. Hell, I told myself, give me enough time and some night she'd let me pull the shades down for her.

"Coffee later, Johnny?"

"Yeah."

1

She went back to her buzzers, her slim fingers dancing over the board. She wasn't any raving beauty. She just looked innocent and interesting. Her hair was black and her eyes were black and she had a pink rose complexion. She also had an hourglass figure with round, soft curves that wobbled just right when she walked—and got me thinking all wrong.

A drunk came in and tried to get the key to somebody else's room. I gave him the right key and he went off toward the elevator, swearing and stumbling. I kicked the stool out of the way and started counting the cash in the drawer.

It was a damn shame for a guy to be caught in a mouse trap like the Hotel Shelly.

The redhead came down from two-four and tossed her body outside. I got the cash mixed up and started all over again.

The only difference between the Hotel Shelly and the city dump was that the hotel had a roof over it. Besides, the dump was out past the edge of town—past Clarke Street, even. Every time I thought of Clarke Street my feet felt like they were stuck in a couple of piles of sand. Clarke Street was the beginning of one world and the end of another.

"You ought to go down and see your folks some night," Janet said. "They'd be glad to see you."

She told me the same thing every night.

"To hell with it," I said.

I told her the same thing every night.

There was no sense for me to knock on the door of number eight Clarke Street. That place was so crowded now there wouldn't be room enough for me to stand inside on one foot. My brother Sam and his wife and four kids had moved in the same day I'd checked out. They only had five rooms on the second floor. The way my old man snored they'd have to sleep with their heads stuck out of the windows. They were welcome to it.

I closed up the cash sheet for my shift and thought about number thirty-seven Clarke Street. That was the big apartment house at the corner of Clarke and Main. That was a tear in another piece of cloth. That was where Julie Wilson lived.

The last time I'd seen Julie she'd been pushing the baby carriage down Main, her slim body looking good in a thin summer dress, her blonde hair cascading over her square-set shoulders, her chin plenty stubborn and her eyes defiant.

"Hello, Julie," I'd said.

The late evening shadows had been falling off the tops of the buildings into the street and she'd looked at me for a second or so before she knew who I was. "Hello, Johnny Reagan," she'd said. And, then, she'd leaned down, looking at the kid, a slight smile pulling at her full lips.

"He looks like me, Johnny."

"Yeah." It'd been getting so dark that I couldn't tell if the kid had one or two heads. "Yeah," I said, "she looks like you all right."

"*He*," Julie said. "He's my boy."

"Okay."

She'd gone on down the street, passing under the light, and I could see that she was walking real straight, like she didn't care. I'd watched her for a long time, thinking about what a lot of guts she had. She wasn't crying, or yelling for the army to bring her sergeant back and make him marry her. She was just living it out to the end of the string.

Fairweather, the other clerk, came on at five of eleven. He was forty-five and as bald as a tennis ball in the sun. He got a bottle out of the cash drawer, went behind the key rack and made a lot of noise with his nose. When he came back I could see some brown spots down the front of his white shirt. Maybe he looked like hell, but there was one thing about him—he was one hundred percent for the hotel and that helped make up for the fifty percent I lacked.

I had to stick around until after he checked the cash. He put on a pair of five-and-ten-cent store glasses and looked everything over like he had a first mortgage on the place. I was getting a whole lot tired of Fairweather.

"On the button," he said, after a while.

I went through the lobby and out to the street. Janet was down at the corner talking with a big, fat man. The white polo shirt the man was wearing hung on him like a burlap bag. I lit a cigarette and walked toward them.

"I want you to meet Mr. Connors," Janet said, tossing her curls. "Mr. Connors, Johnny Reagan."

"Hello," I said.

The fat man grunted and I felt a big, warm hand wind around five of my fingers.

"Mr. Connors is in the insurance business," Janet told me.

We struggled briefly and I got my hand back.

"Life insurance," Connors said.

"That's a tough racket," I said.

"I have agents working for me," Connors explained. "Six of them. I don't do any of the collecting any more myself."

"Well, that's different."

"And it isn't a racket," he insisted. "It's a good way of making a living."

"Sure."

All the insurance men I'd ever known had had big cars—fast and often.

"Johnny works in the hotel," Janet said. "On the desk."

I gave her a hard look; I didn't like to be reminded about the crumby job I had.

"Once I get myself a better deal," I said, "I'm pulling out of that Siberia."

"I know they don't pay much," Connors said.

"You can say that again."

"A young fellow ought to have a better job than that."

Sure, I thought, thirty-one, and five years worse off than if I'd stayed in the box factory. The box factory hadn't paid much, either, but there was always somebody around who could punch the clock for you and build up overtime. At the hotel you could work until they swept you up off the floor and they wouldn't even give you a bottle of beer for your trouble.

"Supposing I wanted to get in the insurance business?" I asked Connors. "How would I go about it?"

He tried to tuck his shirt into his pants but he couldn't quite make it.

"You might just as well come right out and ask me for a job," he said.

"Maybe I will."

"No hedging with you, Johnny."

"It wouldn't get me anyplace, if I did."

He was silent for a couple of minutes, looking me over real good. His face was fat but there was something strong about it, too. Maybe it was his eyes, small eyes that seemed to pull you right up against him. He was a couple of inches shorter than I was, probably six feet, and he held his head back a little, staring up at me.

"I guess you're used to meeting the public, Johnny?"

A guy meets the public in a hotel, in bars, in the box factory, on Clarke Street. The public is people and people are all over, crawling around the world like mice on a box of cheese. A guy can't help stumbling over them.

"I'm used to meeting the public," I assured him.

"And selling? Ever do any selling, Johnny?"

When I was twelve I'd done a little selling for Mae, who'd lived down at the end of Clarke Street, about a yard of cinders away from the railroad. I'd gone up to Main, about ten at night, wandering along the sidewalk and asking all the guys I met all the questions Mae had told me to ask. Mae had been a whore and the cops had run me in for being a kid pimp. I'd given up selling right away.

"I never had a chance," I told him. "I got stopped before I ever got started."

He nodded and lit a cigar as long as my right leg. The smoke from it smelled good in the damp June night. Janet coughed once and waved the blue cloud away from her face. She had a nice smile and clear white teeth. She was a fairly good looking head.

"Tell you what," Connors said. "Why don't you come down to my office in the morning and we'll talk this thing over."

"Thanks," I said. "I will."

"I think one of my men has made up his mind to quit and there might be a possibility for you."

"That would be a good break, all right."

"No promises," he said. "But we can both think about it."

"Sure."

I didn't have to think about it. All he had to do was wave a job at me and I'd knock him down on my way to work.

He gave Janet a big, friendly hug and said goodnight. He went across the street and got into a Cadillac that had wire wheels and lots of chrome. The engine ripped a hole in the night as he shot off up the street.

"Thanks, Janet," I said quietly. "Thanks a hell of a lot."

She looped her arm through mine and crept in close. She had a soft, round hip and I didn't try to push her away. We walked slowly through the alternate patches of light and shadow.

"You might get a good job out of Mr. Connors," Janet said.

"Yeah."

"He seemed to like you."

We kept on walking. The top of her head, about five-feet-two from the ground, hung down there below my left shoulder. All around me was the good, clean freshness of her.

"I was wondering how you knew him," I said. "A big guy with plenty of money."

"I guess he's got money."

"Are you kidding?"

"He used to come to Rotary," she said. "That was last winter, when Rotary met at the hotel and before they decided to go out to Cranberry Inn. He had lots of calls and I tried to be nice to him."

"I guess you were."

She squeezed my arm tight.

"I hope it pays off all right for you," she said.

Up the street a flashing neon light said Pawn Shop. Past that, on the other side, a lighted arrow pointed the way to the

Emergency Finance Company. I wondered how many times my old man had gone up there and hocked his soul.

We turned down a side street and the night was a deeper black.

Janet lived on the third floor of a big brick building in the middle of the block. I had a room in a cracker box a little further down Center Street, two or three smells away from the tannery shed. Both places looked hulking and miserable against the gray night sky.

"It's a hell of a way to live," I said. "Like a rat in the bottom of an empty barrel."

"It's your own fault," she said. "With me it's different. I don't have anybody, but you've got a family."

Janet's father had shot her mother when she was just a little kid, and the father had stuck his head in the gas oven. An aunt had brought her up, but the aunt had died during Janet's last year in high school.

"Damn place looks like a tomb," I told her; there wasn't a light visible from within the brick house.

"They all go to bed real early," she said. "Most of them have to be on the job before eight every morning."

"I suppose so."

We went up the wooden steps to the long, wide porch. The low roof leaned out into the night and pulled the blackness inside. We stumbled over a floor mat and I swore softly.

"'Night, Johnny," she said.

I could feel her right there, real close, and I didn't want her to go away.

"We should have stopped and had a beer," I said. "I sure as hell don't want to go to sleep just yet."

"You're thinking about tomorrow morning, I guess."

Her hand slid up my chest and across my face. I could feel my beard crackle against the soft touch of her fingers.

"Maybe I'm thinking about something else," I said.

A train whistle squalled in the night and a dog started to bark. Somebody next door swore loudly at somebody else and then things got quiet again.

"You're a funny guy, Johnny," Janet said softly. "You talk so tough sometimes—so hard—and you aren't hard at all."

She could take me any way she wanted to.

"I'll be thinking of you in the morning," she said. "And wishing you luck."

She stood on her toes and reached up and pulled my head down. Her lips were dry and afraid and she just pushed them up against my cheek and let go again.

"Plenty of luck, Johnny!" she whispered.

My arms went around her hard and quick and I felt her whole body stiffen. Her back was warm and soft and the taut strap of her brassiere grew more rigid under my thumb.

"Janet, baby!"

She tried to turn her head away but I was too fast for her. My lips found her mouth without any trouble at all. My one hand slid down to the small of her back, just above the round-ness, and I slammed her to me. The heat from her breasts burned through my shirt and blazed twin dots on my chest.

Her lips parted and a tiny sob came up from her throat. Her fingers kneaded my flesh, moving around, and her tongue flashed wild and hot.

"Johnny!"

She began to cry. She was afraid and I knew she was afraid. She was falling apart inside.

I pushed the door open.

"I'll follow you," I said. "I won't make any noise."

"No!"

I kissed her again and she didn't try to get away. But she wouldn't open her mouth any more and the tears were wet on her face.

"Don't turn on the light," I told her. "Just hang onto my hand."

I couldn't see her there in the darkness, but I could feel her trembling.

"Johnny?"

"Yes."

"I—"

She didn't say anything more. Her voice died off into a whimper and she walked on into the house. Her fingers felt cold as she held tight to my hand.

We went up the first flight of stairs and along another hallway. Somebody was snoring in one of the rooms and another guy was talking in his sleep. There was a fifteen-watt bulb at the bottom of the second set of stairs. We slid by that and kept right on going up.

She unlocked her door and we went inside. It was as black as the inside of a bag in there and I couldn't tell very much about the place.

"I think I'm going to hate myself for this tomorrow," she said.

"Tomorrow's a long ways off."

"Maybe it won't come."

"Maybe."

She took me across the room and we sat down on the bed. We sat real close, sliding down into the hollow of the old mattress.

"I'm almost afraid," she said.

"You needn't be."

"It's the first—time."

I pulled her around roughly, jamming my mouth down on her lips. She'd stopped her crying and I was glad of that. Her hair fell against my face and her mouth opened up and the night began.

I got hold of her sweater and ripped it off her.

"You're hurting me, Johnny!"

I hooked my finger under the brassiere strap and the thing popped open.

I touched her breasts and her little flat stomach. Her fingers clawed at my clothes and I heard a button strike the wall. My hand kept going down. She kissed me once more, real hard, and then she flung herself back on the bed, moaning.

"Janet?"

"Yes?"

"If you're afraid—"

"It's all right," she murmured. "I'm not afraid."

I bent and kissed her again. Her arms coiled around my neck, making my shoulders ache. She clung to me with a passion that made me weak, made me almost sick, made me want to die right there in that room.

I pulled the shades down for her that night.

CHAPTER II

Morning After

I SAT on the arm of a chair, staring out of the window at the newness of the morning, seeing nothing. I didn't even bother looking at her. I knew that she was in bed, with the sheet pulled up around her chin, hiding herself like I didn't know what was underneath. Right then, I didn't much care.

"You'd better wait until after the others leave for work," she said.

"Yeah."

"It wouldn't seem right, you going out of here at this time of the morning."

"How'd they know what room I just left?"

She was quiet for a long time, so I turned and looked at her. Her hair slashed a dark ribbon across the white pillow. Her face was flushed and her eyes had a sparkle to them. She smiled and stretched.

"I guess they wouldn't," she said. She puckered up her nose and dug down into the bed. "Anyway, I wouldn't care an awful lot. It would be different if we didn't love each other."

I just stared at her.

She rolled over on her side, facing the wall, and I watched one finger trace a lazy design on the wallpaper.

"It is love, isn't it, Johnny?"

I got up and walked around the chair a couple of times. I couldn't remember everything I'd told her. I was pretty sure that I'd only told her all of the things that any man would tell any woman he happened to take to bed.

"I'd want to be sure, Johnny. I'd want to be awful sure."

"Yeah."

She sat up in bed. The sheet slid down and lay across her hips. Her nightgown dipped away from her breasts, and the hollow between them appeared deep and warm.

"Promise me something, Johnny?"

"Sure."

I offered her a cigarette, trying to keep my eyes on her face. She shook her head and I dropped the pack on the end table.

"Promise me it won't happen again, Johnny?"

"All right."

"Maybe it's real, Johnny, and maybe it isn't. We ought to know, for sure, before it .happens again."

"Okay."

She bit her lip and stared at the points her toes made in the sheet.

"I just hope nothing happens because of—last night."

I began to sweat. I grabbed up a cigarette, lit it and went over to the chair and sat down. I put my shoes on, jerked the strings tight and tied a good, fast bow knot.

"I gotta breeze out of here," I said. "I can't miss seeing that guy Connors this morning."

"Kiss me before you go."

I kissed her. She arched her back and pulled me nearer. I had a pretty good idea how it was with her. She'd been all alone, almost always, and now she thought she'd found some-body.

"Make it good," she said. "And get the job."

I walked over to the door.

"I'll let you know," I said.

I stepped out into the hall and closed the door. Maybe she'd see me again and maybe she wouldn't.

An old lady was running a vacuum in the lower hall but she didn't bother giving me so much as a glance. I heard her shut the cleaning machine off just as I went down the steps.

It was a good morning, clear, and with gentle puffs of white clouds roaming a blue sky. The leaves on the maples were a cool green and some of the dew from the night before lingered in the air.

When I got to Main I stopped in a diner and had coffee and a hard roll. It was still pretty early, only a few minutes after nine, and I didn't think I ought to get down to see Connors before ten.

I had another coffee and kidded the waitress about it going to be a hot day.

"I don't care how hot it gets," she said. "As long as the flies stay out of here. The heat, I dress for that. I don't mind the heat. It's the flies that chase hell out of me."

She had a big body and a little uniform. She was dressed for the heat—and anything else that didn't require much clothes.

I left the diner a few minutes before ten. A little further down Main I stopped in a cigar store and looked up Connors' address in the phone book. I saw that he had a place in town, one out in the country and an office in the five-and-dime building at forty-four Main.

The Connors office was on the second floor, reached by one of those fancy elevators you run yourself. I made a couple of round trips to the basement, prior to stepping off into a rather large waiting room lined with chrome furniture and frosted glass windows.

"Yes, sir?"

The blank face on the opposite side of the counter belonged to a pair of glasses and a fifty-year-old biddy.

"I'd like to see Mr. Connors," I said.

She tried to smile sweetly.

"So would I," she said.

I lit a cigarette and let the smoke wander around her long nose.

"I'm looking for a job," I said.

"I don't know of any here."

"Well, he said there was."

"He ought to know."

"I'll go along with you on that."

The nose carried the glasses away and left me by myself. I picked up a folder that said "Get Nifty—Be Thrifty." I didn't read any of it. I could see that it was just a lot of crap about why a guy should hock his life to an insurance company so that he could die, some day, on a full stomach.

"Mr. Connors isn't in this morning."

I glanced up, ready to swear, but I didn't get around to doing it. I wasn't looking at any phony glasses or long nose or anything like that. What I saw was a piece of blonde dynamite, supercharged with a pair of bright red lips and deep blue eyes.

"Well, Julie," I said. "What the hell are you doing here?"

"Working."

I thought about Clarke Street, and Julie and her kid without any father.

"That's good," I said.

"My third week." Those wet, red lips parted in a smile. "I like it fine."

She had on a thin blouse and she was just tall enough for her breasts to point straight out at me across the counter top. Every time she breathed, they moved. And every time they moved, the more I watched them.

"Mr. Connors won't be in at all today," Julie said. "He called this morning and said he wouldn't be in for the rest of the week."

"The lousy liar!"

Julie studied her unpolished fingernails, picking them together.

"You can't talk that way around here," she said. "All these people have got some class. You aren't back on Clarke Street, Johnny."

"I'm not crying about that."

"Clarke Street isn't so bad," she said. "It's how you live that counts."

I thought about Janet and the night before.

"I'm living," I said.

"Besides, Mr. Connors didn't lie to you, Johnny. Mr. Connors doesn't lie. He's one of the nicest men I've ever known."

"You're beating a hole right through my heart," I said.

Her eyes clouded over and she stopped smiling. She started to say something, but one of the phones inside screamed and she went over to answer it. Beyond where she stood, leaning over a desk and writing something on a pad, I could see some typewriters and adding machines and a couple of more girls.

I could see Julie's legs and they were sleek and trim, sliding up like little columns into the form-fitting folds of a thin pink skirt. I could remember how I'd watched those legs go up and down Clarke Street—when she was ten, when she was fifteen, when she was so damned beautiful that I looked the other way. I remember how I'd tried to get at her, once at night and once when we'd been swimming, and how she'd chased me off every time.

She put the phone down, wrote some more on the paper, and then came back to the window. Her curves didn't miss any loose movements and I didn't miss any of her curves.

I began to wish I'd never seen her again.

"You know where Willow Lake is, Johnny?"

"Yeah," I said.

"Mr. Connors has a place out there. He's moved out there for the rest of the summer."

"Well, good for him."

"When he called this morning he said to have you come out about two this afternoon."

Willow Lake was six miles from town. I wondered how I was supposed to get there.

"His daughter's going to stop around for the mail about one-thirty, and if you're here at the office at that time you can ride out with her."

"Okay."

Things were looking better. If the old guy wasn't interested in me he wouldn't be going to all this trouble.

"You won't get mad if I say something, will you, Johnny?"

"Why should I get mad?"

One of her hands slid across the counter and touched, only briefly, the green sleeve of my sport shirt.

"Wear something better than this, Johnny."

I looked down at the shirt. It really wasn't green any longer, just a sort of pale green-blue shade that looked as though somebody had scrubbed it out on a pile of rocks. I'd been washing the thing days and wearing it nights to keep from running around naked.

"Yeah," I said.

My pants weren't much better. Almost anybody could see, even without looking for it, the press-on patch I'd slapped on the right knee, inside, to keep the leg of the pants from falling off into the street.

"Yeah," I said again. "Thanks. I didn't know I looked so like a crumb."

"Now, don't go getting sore!"

"I'm not."

Her blue eyes grew deep and solemn. The red tip of her tongue came out and moistened her lips. I could hear her breathing, full and unsteady.

"I don't know why I do things like this," she said. "I should keep my big mouth shut. But you can't go out to see Mr. Connors the way you look."

"I can't take these clothes off," I said.

"Another pair of slacks and a nice shirt hadn't ought to cost too much."

"It wouldn't."

"You ought to be able to afford that."

I figured what I had in my wallet. I had something back at the hotel I had to take care of.

"If they started charging me for air this minute," I told her, "I'd drop dead."

She shook her head and turned away.

"You're always broke, Johnny."

"I didn't have anything to start with."

"And neither did I."

She went over to one of the desks and yanked a drawer open. She lifted up some papers and took out her pocketbook. She dug around inside, removed something, then put the pocketbook back in the drawer and closed it.

She was a good kid. She had a buck.

"There's thirty dollars here," she said, sliding her little fist across the counter. "That ought to help you some."

"Maybe I won't get the job."

Her eyes were steady.

"You'll pay it back, Johnny."

I dropped the bills into my shirt pocket.

"Sure," I said. "I'll pay you back."

She didn't ask me when and I didn't try to tell her. I thanked her, gave her another good look and left.

I went down to Barney's at the corner of Main and West. I got a pair of slacks for fourteen ninety-five, a shirt for five bucks and a pair of shoes for eleven dollars. Barney had some sport coats on sale for seventeen-fifty, not bad looking, and I got a gray one with brown dots to go with the brown slacks.

"Must be rolling in dough," Barney said.

"I haven't seen so much money since I got my army bonus," I told him.

"Guys like you," he said, "oughta see more money. You spend it, Johnny."

"Like water."

I had lunch in a dump opposite the railroad station. The prices in Nick's were so low that if you got a roach with your dinner he charged you extra.

"Mighty sharp," Nick said.

"Get your damned dirty hands off my coat!"

"Okay. Okay." He lifted the white apron from around his knees and wiped the sweat from his round face. "Who you studdin' for tonight, Johnny?"

"Shut up!"

I went back to Connors' office shortly after one. I looked around for Julie but I didn't see her, so I guessed that she was out to lunch. The old bag with the nose was arguing with some policy-holder about an overdue premium and stuff like that. I threw a road block across my ears and sat down. Wearing the coat, I felt hotter than a stove lid in the sun.

About one-thirty the door opened up and a girl came in. She was a real tall girl with dark hair and an unimportant face. There wasn't anything wrong with her face, not actually, only it didn't leave much of a first impression. Maybe that was because she wasn't wearing any lipstick or other make-up, just the slight tan that had been given her by the outdoors.

"Mr. Reagan?"

"Yes."

I got up. I looked down at her. She was a couple of inches under six feet and not filled out any more than nature intended.

"My name is Beverly. Beverly Connors."

"Glad to know you."

"Dad asked me to pick you up here and lug you out to Willow Lake."

The way she talked, I might as well have been a sack of potatoes. I guessed that she'd gone to Vassar, or some other snob school.

"Okay, Miss Connors."

"You're all ready?"

I had my shoes on and my teeth were brushed. What the hell else did she want?

"Sure."

I let her operate the elevator because I didn't want to take a chance on it going down into the cellar again. She knew her buttons all right and we got to the first floor without any trouble.

A yellow Packard convertible, with the top down, was parked at the curb.

"Won't you get in?"

She didn't have to write me an invitation. I got in, sinking up to my stomach in cushion.

I got a glance of a long, straight leg as she slid in behind the wheel. I could tell, the way her dress lay across her thighs, that her legs were a lot better than some of the rest of her.

"Dad won't be home until around five," she said. The Packard lurched out into the traffic and the heat funneled around the windshield. "He wanted me to invite you to stay for dinner tonight, so that you could talk later."

I was supposed to be at the hotel desk at four.

"Would it be too much trouble to stop by the Shelly Hotel?" I asked her. "I ought to tell them I'll be late."

"Glad to."

"Thanks."

There was something else I had to do, too. Somebody might give that guy in nine-four a bill and then the roof would blow off the place.

"Mr. Reagan, I was talking to you."

"Oh? Sorry!"

"I was asking you if you swim?"

"Why, sure."

The wind dropped inside of the car and did things with her skirt.

"Daddy suggested that I might entertain you while you're waiting for him."

"That's nice of you."

She smiled and threw her head back, letting her hair fall wild across her shoulders.

"That means we go swimming, Mr. Reagan."

"Okay."

"You ought to pick up your suit, then. There aren't any extra ones out there."

I didn't own a suit. The last time I'd gone swimming I hadn't needed a suit. And neither had the girl.

"Forget about the hotel," I told her. "Just stop by Barney's and I'll get myself a pair of trunks."

"Fine!"

I gave her a big grin and casually lit a cigarette.

CHAPTER III

Jail Bait

WILLOW LAKE is one of those summer resorts where the rich come in June to stay all summer, and where the poor come in July or August to spend two weeks—and manage to survive one.

"It's beautiful, isn't it, Johnny?"

It was late in the afternoon, around four, and by this time we'd got around to calling each other Johnny and Beverly. We were lying on a raft, about fifty feet off shore, soaking up the sun.

"Nothing like it."

I sat up, yawning, and looked around. The surface of the lake was wide and silver, ringed with dark green pines. The shoreline was studded with sandy beaches and all sorts of little and big houses. At the extreme end a motorboat cut a white swath through the water.

"You're from Middlesville, aren't you, Johnny?"

"Yes."

"What part?"

I thought about Clarke Street, where people slept four to a bed, where a couple of white fellows lived with colored girls, where the cops walked in pairs at night.

"Just town," I said.

The raft jiggled and I knew that she was rolling over. She'd been doing that all afternoon, first one way and then the other, letting the sun burn her an even shade of brown. I'd looked at her a lot, trying to get interested, but I hadn't had much luck.

"All the time?" she asked. "Were you born there?"

"Sure."

"So was I."

Well, I thought, good for her.

"But I haven't lived there very much for a long time," she said. "Just during the summer months."

"Away to school?"

"That's right."

"And you go back in September?"

"I'm all finished," she said. "Isn't that nice?"

"I guess so."

"And I didn't learn a thing."

The motorboat swung wide at the end of the lake, turning toward us, plowing a wide furrow in the water.

"Well," I said, "maybe you don't have to know anything."

Her old man had plenty of money and she wasn't the worst looking head in the state. She'd do all right for herself.

"Maybe you're right, Johnny," she said, standing up. "Perhaps I don't have to know anything. Only what I want."

I got up, feeling the hot sun on my body.

"We ought to be getting in," I said. "I don't want to keep your father waiting."

She nodded and pulled the red cap down over her hair. Her suit, a one piece thing, matched the color of her cap. She filled it out pretty good all over, and I began to wonder if I hadn't been somewhat wrong about her.

Her legs flashed brown in the sun and she cut the water like the sharp point of a knife. I waited until she came up for air and then I went in after her, traveling fast.

I beat her to the shore and she laughed about that.

"With those shoulders of yours," she said, "you ought to be able to swim all day."

I gave her a grin and took her arm as we went up through the deep sand.

The Connors summer home was a big place, long and rambling. All of the rooms were on one floor, arranged in sort of a square, and these were connected by a wide, screened-in porch.

"You know where your room is, Johnny?"

"Yeah."

She padded off across the porch and I went down to one of the corner rooms. It was a large room with a double bed and maple furniture. The wide window pointed straight at the lake.

I took a shower in the tiled bath and rubbed down good. I'd just put my shorts on when somebody knocked on the door.

"Yes?"

"Would you like a drink, Johnny?"

What I wanted to do was see Connors, find out about the job, and get the hell back to the hotel. Clerking wasn't my life's work but I didn't have this other job yet and it was better than nothing.

"Dad got back," Beverly said, "but he's gone down to the lake for a dip. He said you might like a drink while you're waiting."

"Well, then, I'll take a beer."

"Sure?"

"Positive." I tried to put my socks on but I had to dry my feet some more. "I usually drink beer."

"Okay."

I got into the rest of my clothes, slung the coat over my arm and went outside. I saw her suit hanging on the porch railing, so I draped mine beside it.

She came along the porch, carrying a tray. There was a bottle of beer and a couple of highballs on it.

"We'll go around to the terrace," she said, handing me the tray.

I'd never seen a terrace before, not that I knew about, but I found out that it was nothing more than a lot of rocks thrown around on top of the ground. The small space was crowded with a couple of tables and some wicker furniture. A gray-haired woman lounged in one of the chairs, her head thrown back, her eyes closed.

"Mother," Beverly said, "I'd like you to meet Johnny Reagan. Johnny, my mother."

The woman slowly opened her eyes and blinked at the sun. I had the feeling that she'd closed them just a couple of seconds before we got there.

"How do you do?" she wanted to know, pulling herself up out of the chair.

"Okay," I said.

Mrs. Connors was a short, skinny woman with dark eyes and a trace of fuzz across her upper lip. She was wearing purple shorts and a yellow halter that sagged away from her loose breasts. I didn't like her for sour apples.

"Good swim?" she wanted to know.

"Very good," Beverly said. She poured the beer and it foamed up over the top of the glass. "Johnny's pretty sharp in the water."

Her mother grunted and put the highball away without fooling around about it.

"Well," she said, "I've got to go and see about dinner. I wish I could get help that would stay out here in the sticks in the summer. Becky got mad and quit again."

"Oh, no!" Beverly tasted her drink and glanced at me. "Isn't that horrible?"

I agreed that it was.

"Stupid help!" Beverly complained, after her mother had gone. "They can stay out here all summer, living just like us. You'd think that they'd appreciate it. But they don't. They're just—stupid!"

I drank the beer and made some mental rules as concerned the Connors family. I had no opinion about the old guy himself, but I had a great big idea about mother and daughter. Anything that might happen to them was all right with my conscience.

We talked some more and she swung her long legs around but I didn't pay any attention to them. I was getting a little tired of her company by the time Connors came up from the lake.

The water ran down off his fat stomach and splashed onto the terrace. His chest was big, almost like a woman's, only covered with thick gray hair.

"Have a drink, Daddy?"

He gave Beverly a pat across her backside. She jumped and he laughed at her.

"Your hand's all wet!"

"If you wore some clothes," he said, "you wouldn't know it."

Her face colored slightly and she swung away from him.

"You run along," he said. "Maybe you can help your mother. Johnny and I have something we want to talk about."

She gave me a smile before she left.

"Don't let him do all of the talking," she warned. "He will, if you give him a chance."

Connors stared after his daughter until she disappeared around a corner of the house. Then he shook his head, laughing, and sat down in one of the chairs. The frame of the wicker shifted over to a precarious angle and hung there.

"Great girl," he said, with pride. "Great pal."

"Yeah."

"Only child," he went on. "Not spoiled. Not spoiled a bit."

"No."

He could think any way he wanted. He was paying for it.

He talked about the lake, and this house, and how long he'd been coming out there every summer. The sun burned across my face and I began to get sleepy.

"It's been a good life," he said. "And it's come out of the life insurance business. Every bit of it."

I tried to wake up.

"That's the way I had it figured," I said. "A man can make his own goal when he's selling. Nobody's going to tell him to take it easy and not do so much."

"You're right, Johnny."

"You wouldn't tell me I could only write so many policies. Instead, you'd tell me to get out there and get more."

"I guess you have the general idea."

"And you'd be doing me a favor," I said. "Because I'd be making more. We'd both be making more."

He told me about some of his agents and what they didn't want to do and why they didn't want to do it. It was obvious that I'd said the correct thing and every time he gave me a chance I said some more of the same.

"You talk like you might fall right into it," Connors said, after a while. He squinted his eyes into the sun, following the movement of a canoe in the middle of the lake. "That's why I asked you up here today. I had the same thoughts last night."

"Thanks."

"Funny how you can decide something so quickly."

"Yeah."

He stood up, rubbing the palms of his hands against his eyes.

"We've got a routine questionnaire down at the office that would have to be filled out," he said. "But you hadn't ought to have any trouble with that. Never had any—money troubles, have you?"

"I've been broke."

"I mean, never swiped any money, have you?"

"No."

"That'll be all right, then. Of course, we'll check where you've worked, and like that, but there shouldn't be any question about it. You can have the job if you want it."

"Thanks."

"You'd start at sixty a week, plus commissions."

"Not bad."

He went around the house and I followed him.

"I'm going in to town after dinner," Connors said. "I'd like to have you eat with us and I'll take you in when I go."

I thought about the hotel and how something might happen before he checked on me the next day.

"Maybe I could use the phone?"

"Help yourself," he said. "You'll find it in back of the third door, down."

"Thanks."

I was getting tired of thanking him. He hadn't done much for me yet.

"There's liquor in there, too," he said. "And beer in the Coke box. Help yourself. I drink quite a lot, so don't think I'll hold it against you."

"I'll keep that in mind."

He shuffled off, his weight making some of the boards squeak. I went to the third door and pushed it open. I saw that it was a play room with a pool table, record player and a slot machine. The Coke case was over in one corner, and, above that, several shelves loaded with liquor.

I got the hotel on the phone right away, but it wasn't Janet who answered. It was the day operator and she sounded as though her temperature was up fifteen degrees.

"Let me talk to Janet," I said.

"She ain't here."

"This is Johnny."

"Where the hell are you?"

"I wanted to talk to Janet," I said. "But maybe I can leave a message."

"Not with me," she said. "Janet doesn't work here any more. She got herself fired."

"What?"

"Just as she was coming on, too. Another five minutes and I'd have been out of this trap. She comes in when this guy is up at the desk, wanting to check out, and saying that he was paid up for the whole week. They're blaming you and saying you're a crook, when up walks Janet, big as life, and says she did it. So they fired her. Beats me why she'd—"

I put the phone back on the cradle and lit a cigarette. I noticed that my hands were shaking. Then I went across the room and jerked up the lid on the Coke box.

I didn't have anything to worry about.

CHAPTER IV

Desire

CONNORS ate enough steak for five ditch diggers and it gave him a good case of jumping stomach. Afterward, we went out on the porch and gave the mosquitoes a chance to grab themselves a transfusion.

"Maybe I ought to see a doctor," Connors said, belching.

"That might be a good idea," I said.

He was sprawled out in one of those low slung canvas deck chairs that look like they'll collapse almost any second. Beverly got him a big glass of Bromo-Seltzer and I tried to figure out, while he was drinking it, where he had room to put it. I guess maybe he didn't, though, because he started burping like a firecracker in wet grass.

"I thought you were going to take Mr. Reagan in to town," Mrs. Connors said when she joined us. "Perhaps he has something he wants to do."

She was damned right I had something to do. Janet might have got herself sacked on account of me, not yelling, but she was apt to get thinking it over, later, and decide to square herself with the hotel. If she pulled a fancy stunt like that I wouldn't be able to use them for a reference. And I couldn't use the factory, the place I'd worked before, because I'd gotten next to the boss's wife too fast and too often. Hell, it hadn't been my fault that she'd hung out around the shipping room, looking for something all the time—and finding it real easy. But that didn't make any difference, except that I wouldn't be able to get a say-so from the little runt on any job I was trying to get. And the job before that, the one in the restaurant checking in supplies, that was a sad bit of business, too. She'd been at least forty and I wouldn't have undressed her with the pot washer's hands. The only thing, the pot washer had been doing it all right and when he'd slid away into the night without leaving a forwarding address, she'd coyly waved her finger under my nose. And I'd waved right back at her. From the door. On the way out.

"Perhaps Beverly would run you in," Connors said to me. He swung his head around to look up at his daughter. "Would you mind doing that?"

"Of course not."

"Sorry as hell, Johnny, but I—"

"Oh, that's okay."

"And you might stop at the baker's," Mrs. Connors told Beverly. "I'd like a cake made for Thursday of next week."

"Bridge again?"

"Yes, dear."

"Hell!"

Beverly went inside and Mrs. Connors told me she didn't know what this generation was coming to. I told her I didn't, either. Which was the truth. Anything could happen.

Beverly was gone about fifteen minutes but it was almost worth the investment of even my time. She had put on a tight fitting skirt and an off-the-shoulder blouse. And I mean it was off the shoulder, almost down to her elbows. But the front of it was a farce because it went just so low and no further.

I remembered how flat she'd looked up there that afternoon and that she hadn't been much better in the bathing suit. I made up my mind that she'd either put on a different style bra or she'd graduated to falsies, because she wasn't flat any more. Real or not, she had plenty up there now to push around.

"I wish you wouldn't wear clothes like that," Mrs. Connors said as Beverly sauntered across the porch. "It's almost indecent."

If the old lady could have her way she'd most likely throw her kid into a tin barrel and hitch a lock onto it.

"Oh, let her alone," Connors said.

I told them goodnight, that I'd enjoyed the dinner and that they sure had a swell joint out in the sticks.

"Come down to the office in the morning and fill out those papers," Connors said as I went down the steps. "Say, around nine-thirty."

"Okay. And thanks, again."

"Don't mention it."

I followed the girl to the car and got in. She started the thing and swung out the driveway. I leaned back and lit a cigarette, wondering where I'd find Janet and how I'd handle her after I did.

"I love a convertible," Beverly said, pulling onto the main road. "Don't you?"

"Sure thing."

"They make the summer so much more alive."

"Yeah."

The sun burned red in the sky, dying fast. It was almost as though the sky had busted an artery, spewing out crimson blood all over the maples and the pines. I glanced at the girl beside me, trying to figure her right. At first she'd seemed tall and a whole lot gawky, but now she was just tall and not too hard to look at. I don't mean that she was pretty—she could get herself a new plastic job and she'd never be pretty—but she wasn't exactly repulsive, either. There was something inside of her, though, that made her a lot different than most girls I'd known. I could tell, easy, that she was trying to act prim all the time and that she was smoking plenty around the edges. If she'd wanted to be rich-bitchy nice she wouldn't put on such a tight skirt or a blouse that was hardly big enough to cover up an idea. Of course her folks waded around in ten dollar bills all the time and she'd been to some fancy school, so that probably had something to do with it. But it would take more than those two things to keep her fastened down once she decided to break herself loose.

"What kind of a car have you got?" she wanted to know.

"I haven't got any."

"That'll make it hard for you selling insurance."

"I guess I can walk for a while."

"Sometimes people aren't home. You have to keep going back."

"So I'll just walk some more," I told her. Or, I thought, I'll get a pair of roller skates—a pair of roller skates and a broom to ride. "Maybe they'll feel sorry for me," I said. "After I wear four inches off my legs they might wake up and pay on time."

She laughed, throwing her head back for a moment, and I noticed that she had a nice laugh. It wasn't a low laugh, or a sexy one, but it came from down deep, building up, like she felt it and wanted you to share it with her.

"Dad's got a Ford he might lend you," she said. "We don't use it much."

"That would be fine."

She was still smiling and when she glanced at me her eyes had a laughter all of their own.

"You're quite a character, Johnny. Did you know that?"

I gave her a grin and watched the way the wind played around with the top of her blouse.

"I don't know whether to get sore at that or not," I said.

"Well, I don't know why you should."

I started to tell her I was sorry, because I didn't want any trouble with her while her old man was on the hook, but she laughed again and I knew that she was just giving me the needle so I could feel it. That made it all right and I was pretty sure that I didn't have to worry about her at all.

"You don't mind if I tell you something else, Johnny Reagan?"

"No."

"You're a most—unusual man."

"Is that so?"

"I really mean that. I didn't mean it about you being a character."

"Well, thanks."

We were getting close to town and as we met approaching cars I noticed that they bothered her. She'd haul the Packard way off to the right and a couple of times I thought we were going to go into the lumber business. Even in a car as big as the Packard those trees looked mighty rugged. I felt like saying something to her about it, but I didn't. I just sat there and got nervous.

"Most of the men I've met," she said, making another pass at the ditch, "were fellows with upper-blood around here, or at college."

I didn't know what she meant by upper-blood but I had a pretty good idea. She meant somebody with a quart instead of two pints.

"I can understand that," I told her.

"And they all seem so—weak."

I'd known a guy in the army, a fellow by the name of Jigger, who'd been left a half million bucks by an uncle in Yonkers. We'd been separated after we'd been shipped out of the States but I'd hauled myself around there as soon as I'd been discharged. Only he hadn't been at home, just his wife, a little English girl with a nose the size of a ripe pear. She'd sniffled a bit and shown me the letter from Jigger's commanding officer. In plain language the officer had informed her that her husband, Corporal Sam Jigger, had accidentally pulled a pin on a hand grenade, had placed his body thereon and had gone the way of a lot of flesh—up in the air. I'd hung around the English nose for a couple of hours, long enough to find out that the only thing she'd saved had been the letter—she hadn't found a way of spending that—and then I'd left.

"Hey!" I yelled as she swung into North Street, way over, just missing the curb. "You want me to smash a hole in your windshield with my head?"

"Nothing happened," she said, letting up on the gas a little bit. "I was just going too fast, that's all."

"You can say that again."

The way Beverly Connors drove she should have bought a car in the five-and-ten and pulled it along behind her on a string.

"Now I forgot what I was talking about," she complained.

She hadn't been saying anything, so why should she be worried about it?

"Oh, yes! I said they were weak. I wouldn't say the same thing about you." She looked at me straight, not smiling. "I'd say that you're ruthless, Johnny."

"Maybe I am."

"You walk almost like a big jungle cat, almost—well, sort of beautiful and terrible, too."

She didn't really mean that. What she meant was that if I wanted her to pull that convertible into a dark alley she might not start driving the other way. Only I wasn't having any. All I wanted from Connors was a job and a chance to make a fast buck.

"I wish you'd keep your eyes on the road," I told her.

"I am."

"Well, all right."

We were on North Street, coming into the main part of town. The shadows dipped down the tops of the buildings and fell across the street. It wasn't dark and it wasn't dusk, just a sort of in-between. I kept watching the street, hoping that some kid wasn't out there playing around. The way Beverly Connors handled that Packard, a kid wouldn't have a chance. She'd put him in the hospital until he was old enough to graduate.

"Where did you want to get off?"

"Center Street."

"I don't know where that is."

Of course she wouldn't know. Probably some of the money it had taken to buy the Packard had come from Center Street, but that wouldn't be of any concern to her.

"Oh, hell," I said, "just drop me off wherever you get this thing stopped."

That happened to be about a hundred feet further on. There was a busted beer bottle in the street and she didn't see it. The right front tire blew out and Beverly squealed. She hopped onto the brake and we came to a stop alongside the curb.

"Damn!" she said, her face angry. "You'd think people would keep their bottles out of the street."

I got out and stretched.

"Well, it was a good place to knock it off," I said.

We were almost in front of Angie's, a little gin mill not far from Center Street. During the week Angie's was usually pretty quiet, but on Saturday night you could get anything you wanted in there. All you had to do was ask. Or sit and look and it'd come to you.

"You got the keys for the trunk?" I asked her. "I'll change it for you."

She slid across the seat, her dress crawling up her legs, and got out on the sidewalk side.

"There aren't any tools, anyway."

"That's great."

She looked at the red and green neon lights in front of the bar, doubtfully.

"They must have a phone in there."

"Sure."

"I'll call daddy's garage. They'll come over and fix it."

She didn't have to worry about that. That guy would show up even if he had a busted arm and five holes in his head.

She leaned inside the car, stretching, hunting for the keys. Her legs looked a lot better in stockings, the kind with a lot of black on the heels and a dark ridge running all the way up them. But they didn't look good enough for me to cause her any trouble.

We walked down to Angie's and went inside. The bartender behind the bar looked up and pushed his paper underneath. A guy who was sitting in one corner, his glass to his mouth, put his glass down again and gave Beverly a good solid glance. Maybe she looked all right, swinging around that way as she crossed the small dance floor, but I only got a glimpse. I was too busy with something else.

"The phone's in back," I told her.

"I won't be long."

"Take your time."

She could take the whole stinking night and I wouldn't even miss her. Once or twice in the car, coming down, I'd had a little flame lit for her but it hadn't amounted to anything, no more than any woman who's got her teeth and two legs and a couple of other things can do to a man.

I walked down to the end of the bar, feeling the night getting bigger, just letting my eyes wander over her.

"Hello, Johnny."

"Hey, Julie!"

"I see you're not losing any time."

I shrugged and leaned up against the bar beside her. She was sitting on the stool at an angle, her left side to the bar, and her bare legs stuck out all over below her black shorts. She had on a black sweater, one of those loose knit things, and I could see the tiny pink dots of her brassiere staring out at me. I guess she knew what I was interested in because she swung around, facing the bar, and took the view away.

"We had a flat," I said.

"You or her?"

"That isn't nice."

She shrugged and tapped one foot on the bar rail.

"Mr. Connors is pretty much sold on his daughter," she told me. "It might be a good thing if you remember that, Johnny."

I knocked a quarter on the bar. The bartender nodded and drew a beer. He brought it down and left the quarter where it was.

"I'll remember it."

"No fooling."

"Look," I said irritably, "I got no idea of trying to get squatter's rights on that. You ought to know better."

"I know you," Julie said, smiling. "That's enough."

"How come you loaned me that money, then?"

"I don't know." She finished her beer and the bartender came for her glass. "I must be nuts."

She held her hand over the top of her glass, calling it quits, but I told the bartender to give her another one, anyway. Just then Beverly came out from the back. I made up my mind that she'd drink beer or go thirsty. She didn't do either. She ordered gingerale, straight, and the two singles in my pocket got a lot happier.

After a while a truck pulled up in front and we could hear some tools getting banged around. Julie took a nickel and went across to the juke box. She asked me what I wanted to hear and that made me feel good. She'd had a couple of more beers and she might be getting sociable. I went over to her.

"Just play 'I'm in the Mood for Love,' Baby," I told her.

"I'll play what I want."

The light from inside the box outlined where she was filled out, spilling over almost, and I could tell every time she took a breath.

"What the hell," I said, "so why bother asking—"

"I wanted to tell you something. I didn't want her to hear."

"That's different."

"Some girl called the office for you, late this afternoon."

"Yeah?"

"She sounded upset." Julie swung away from the juke box, our eyes meeting briefly. "I thought you'd want to know."

"Thanks."

We went back to the bar and I swallowed the beer in a rush. What I ought to do was to get down to Janet's place and set her straight on a couple of things. I looked at Julie and made up my mind it could wait.

"I guess the car's finished," Beverly said.

A mechanic struck his head inside and waved at her. She waved back and the top of her blouse did the same thing. I ordered another beer. Sometimes she looked pretty good. Hell, sometimes they all looked that way.

"You going?" Beverly wanted to know.

"I just got a refill. It isn't far to walk, anyway."

"I'll see you?"

"Sure."

"Could I catch a ride with you?" Julie asked. "I hate to walk along the street after dark in these shorts."

The way she was built, I didn't blame her. Even a guy's shadow might get interested if he saw her.

"Sure," Beverly said, hesitating. "Drop you anyplace."

Julie slid past me, just touching, and I could feel the bump of one firm breast against my shoulder.

"See you," she said.

"Sure."

They went across the dance floor and those black shorts of Julie's looked like they were going to bust loose at the seam. They were plenty tight and what she had on under them wouldn't stay still. My eyeballs were still jumping around after the door slammed behind them.

"I never seen anything like it," the bartender told me. "The one in the black, she's put together with all her bricks stacked up right."

"No one'll ever call you a liar for that."

"Sometimes I wish I was younger." He thought about that for a moment and his face lighted up. He stared at the door, squinting his eyes. "Say, you know what they tell me? They say that the young ones like 'em older. I heard a girl in here one night telling that. She wasn't over twenty and she kept saying the young guys don't know what it's all about. She had a guy with her older than me and she kept loving him up all the time. Cripes, they had a good time!"

"I'll bet."

"You suppose I could work something like that with this chicken?"

"You could try it."

"Maybe buy her a few drinks." The bartender's voice was thoughtful and his eyes were almost closed. "On my night off I could hang around here, sort of putting in my time. She might come in, like she did tonight, and I could get the relief bartender to fix up the drinks for nothin'. Later on, if she should want some money, why—"

"Knock it off, will you?"

The bartender scowled and shifted his weight around.

"Say, what's chewin' on your insides?"

"Give me two packs of Rheingold, will you?"

"Cans?"

"That's right. Cans. The little ones."

He sighed and looked at the door again.

"You got me all messed up, mister. I almost had it figured how I could get me a little of that."

I was sore and he was right close and I could have belted him. But I didn't. I just took the beer, dropped the two ones onto the bar and left.

In one big way the bartender and Johnny Reagan were a lot different.

He was willing to pay. I wasn't.

CHAPTER V

Kiss and Make Up

THE NIGHT was hot and close, the way it gets before a storm. The beer pushed out through my skin and turned to sweat. I was almost sorry that I'd invested my dough in those twelve cold cans of Rheingold I carried under my arm. I wouldn't be able to drink that stuff for breakfast, not when I had to go downtown and see Connors. But, hell, I had to have something I could work on Janet with. I had to get her on my side and keep her there. Maybe the beer wasn't the most brilliant idea in the world but it was better than some I could think of. Besides, I wouldn't have to worry about having it for morning. There wouldn't be any left.

Just before I got to Center Street a figure moved out of a darkened doorway toward me.

"Hi, Johnny."

I stopped and waited.

"Hello, Buck," I said.

He wasn't drunk but he wasn't feeling too much pain, either. I could smell the cheap wine and garlic. And I could smell him.

"What's new?" I wanted to know.

"You know what," he said.

I did. He was about my age, maybe a couple of years older, and he'd been half shot ever since he'd been ten years old. Maybe his old lady had nursed him on a bottle of hair tonic. I don't know. But I remembered him from high school, how he'd heaved in one of the study halls and how the teacher had her nice new dress all messed up because she'd thought he was sick and tried to hold his head in her lap. He hadn't come back after that one. Saturdays he used to come down to the wholesale fruit markets where some of us worked, asking for money. He always asked for a dollar and we started calling him Buck.

"I thought well of you all the time, Johnny."

"You got something to say, say it."

"I need a dollar. That's all, just a dollar."

I started walking on.

"Lookit, Johnny!" He must have spotted the beer, because he ran after me. "Just one can. How about that? One can."

"I got it for a friend," I said.

He got hold of my shirt and jerked, hard. He started to laugh and his bad breath was worse than something dead. I swung around, pushing him away. The street light down at the corner showed up his face real good and I could see that his teeth were still white. They'd always been white. I couldn't figure it.

"Try the fruit market," I told him.

"I don't know nobody down there no more."

"That's tough. Get acquainted."

"Just one can, Johnny. For Cripes sake!"

"No. I told you, it's for a friend."

"Must be some skirt."

"So what, even if it is?"

"That Wilson dame." He began to come closer, his eyes bugging out at the beer, and he was almost shouting. "That's who it's for. I remember how you used to chase after that. Thought she had her skirts in her hand just for you, didn't you? And she didn't, did she? And now you're buyin' beer for her. You're gettin' her beer and you won't even give me a drink. Ain't that somethin'! You ain't got a beer for an old friend, but you'll lug it down to that whore—"

I didn't hit him very hard. I didn't even take the beer out from under my left arm. I just slugged him with my right, high on the cheekbone and gauging what I put behind the blow, and he went to sleep on somebody's lawn.

I went down to Center Street and turned in. If it wasn't that I might have use for the beer, I'd have thrown it away. That guy back there gave me the jumps. Hell, in two years I could be like that. Anybody could get that way.

There were a lot of lights on in the brick house. I tried to remember which room Janet had, but I couldn't. That didn't matter because there were lights burning in all of them, anyway. I wrapped my arm tighter around the beer, hiding it a little, and walked up onto the porch.

"Hey, mister?"

"Yeah."

A woman got up from a porch chair and shuffled toward me. When she got in front of the door, standing in the light, I could see that she was in her late fifties or early sixties. She had gray hair and her stern appearing face wasn't the easiest thing that I'd looked at in a long time.

"You don't live here, mister. Whatcha doin', goin' inside?"

I didn't like her voice any better; it sounded sharp, like glass falling out of a window.

"Well, mom," I said, trying to soften her up, "I got myself in a little huff with my girl. I wanted to stop around and straighten it out."

"Which girl?"

"Janet."

"The dark haired one? The one up on the third floor?"

"I don't know which floor," I said. "I never been up there."

Her face relaxed and she didn't act quite so tense.

"They sneak in sometimes," she said. "You don't know how it is, runnin' a roomin' house. You get a man in a room and he brings in a woman. You get a woman in a room and a man just naturally follows. It's a hell of a business."

"I don't want to get you in any trouble."

She looked at me closely.

"I don't think you would." She walked around to the other side and punched at the beer. "You shouldn't be takin' that up there. I don't like drinkin' in my rooms."

If the old bag thought I was going to leave it on the porch where she could drink it, she had a rain check coming.

"I wish you'd let me go up," I told her. "I don't want Janet to go on feeling bad."

She circled me, pretending to think it over. A couple of bugs were slamming their brains against the screen and she whacked them aside. A baby next door fretted with the heat and further down the block a girl giggled because somebody wouldn't leave her alone.

"You oughta make it right with me," she said. "I don't usually do these things."

I didn't say anything.

"I'm really doin' you a favor," she went on, staring out at the street. "Your girl's up there and you wanta see her, dontcha?"

"That's the general idea."

"An' you know how it is with me?"

"You just told me that."

"Well—now, mister, look, if you was to give me, say, a five, well—"

I shoved her aside and she bumped up against the house.

"Have fun," I told her.

I went on inside and started up the stairs. I expected her to follow me, or yell, but she didn't. Probably she sat out there on the porch almost every night, watching her deadfall. When it worked, she made a buck. When it didn't work, she didn't lose anything. It was one form of semi-prostitution that I hadn't encountered before.

Janet didn't come to the door right away. In fact, she took so long about doing it that I began to have the idea that she'd gone down to the hotel, squared things away, and that she was back at her switchboard. That's all I'd need. She could short circuit me so fast I wouldn't know where my connections were.

The door opened up slowly and started to close quick.

"Please, Johnny!"

I pushed the door open and walked in.

"You can throw the night latch on," I told her.

She stood leaning up against the closed door, watching me. I put the beer on the dresser and sat down on the bed.

"I guess you're sort of burned up, huh, Janet?"

"I'd rather not talk about it."

"But I think we should."

She didn't move except where she was breathing and there she moved plenty. She had on a thin dressing gown of some yellow material and it didn't look as though she had more than two layers of skin on underneath. The belt was tied and her belly was real flat above the band and bulging out just slightly below it. She had her black hair pulled back and tied up with a ribbon so that it wouldn't be so hot on her neck. Her eyes were dull, like she'd been bawling, and she didn't have any makeup on. She didn't look very happy.

"I'm trying to figure out what happened down at the hotel," I said.

"How do you know anything happened?"

"I called. The day girl they kept on told me about it."

"I feel like a thief," she said, still not moving. "It's awful!"

"Sure."

"I don't know why I did it."

"Maybe you wanted to help me."

"Tell me something," she said. Her voice trembled and her eyes were blazing mad. "How low can you get?"

It wasn't any time to play cat and mouse with her. She was a woman and she was sore and she was apt to do anything. Of course, it would be hard for her to prove that she hadn't taken the money, after she'd admitted it, but somebody might start wondering how she'd gotten her hand in the till in the first place.

"You ought to know that," I said, looking at her straight. "I can get ten dollars low."

She walked across the room slowly, the robe swinging around her legs and rustling.

"I can't understand why you'd take it."

"I needed the money," I said. "Just for last night."

"Because of me?"

I shrugged. She looked into the mirror, patting her face, touching the corners of her eyes with her fingertips.

"Was that the first time?"

"Yeah."

Well, it had been the first time at the hotel, anyway. Nobody else, except that guy, had ever paid in advance. Usually you had to sue them or take their women away in order to get them up to date.

"I'm glad," Janet said.

I got up and went over to the dresser and ripped one of the beer cartons apart. She brushed past me, feeling close and clean, and sat down on the bed. The bartender had given me a can opener and I got that out. The beer was getting warm and it had been bounced around some; it hissed like a snake when I punched the holes in the cans.

"You got any glasses, Janet?"

"I don't often drink beer."

I looked into the mirror and she looked back at me, trying not to smile. Her robe had drifted apart between her legs. She knew what the mirror said and she moved a little, blushing, so that I wouldn't know so much so soon. Things looked pretty good.

"I don't mind the cans if you don't," I said.

"Well—all right."

"One to making things right," I said. "Between us."

She looked back at me via the mirror. This time she smiled.

"Yes, Johnny. The first beer to make it right."

Who could tell what the twelfth one would be for?

We sat on the bed, not too close at first, and the beer ran down her chin when she tried to drink out of the can. She laughed and let me show her how.

"I ought to be mad at you," she said. "But I'm not."

I opened two more cans. She started drinking the second one right away. I decided her nerves had been split apart since the to-do at the hotel and the beer felt good when it washed up against the sharp ends.

"You didn't tell me how you made out with Mr. Connors," she said. She acted like she wanted to fall back, stretching out on the bed, but she didn't do it. She kept sitting up very straight, the way a virgin would sit at a fireman's clambake. "Or are you going back to the hotel? You can, you know."

I didn't tell her where they could put the hotel but she got the general idea. She looked almost happy when I told her about the hole she'd pulled me out of with that ten, and that things appeared to be real hot for the insurance business.

I opened up another beer.

"You're going to think I'm an awful drinker," she said.

"Yeah. A real heller."

"But I'm not."

She wasn't sitting up so straight any more. She sort of leaned off to one side, on her elbow, and the robe wouldn't keep itself closed up. Every couple of minutes she'd put the beer can down on the floor and organize what clothes she had. By the time she took another swallow she was falling apart all over again.

"Well, let's have another one," I said. "Then, I have to get out of here."

She was quiet while I opened up the beer. When I turned around I saw that she'd fixed the pillows, one on top of the other, and that she was lying back against them. She hadn't bothered to cover her legs, not all the way, and up toward the top of the robe she'd been careless, too. She'd taken off the ribbon and her hair spread in black waves across the pillow.

"I don't think I want any more," she said.

I put the beer back on the dresser.

"Maybe I don't, either," I said.

"Johnny?"

"I hear you."

"About last night—"

I started to sweat, looking down at her. The blood and the beer inside me rocked around and threatened to explode.

"What about last night, Janet?"

She stared up at me and smiled. Her lips were full and wet and red. She moved luxuriously, digging down into the bed, and the top of the robe didn't belong to her any more. It was down off her shoulders, away from her, and there was just her flesh, soft and full, waiting for me.

"Let's not let it happen again," she whispered.

I didn't say anything. I couldn't say anything. She'd brought me right up to the curve and then she'd pushed me off the road. It was like falling into a well and then have somebody drop a sandbag onto you.

"All right, Johnny?"

I kept looking down at the floor, away from her.

"Please, Johnny!"

"Okay," I said.

I thought about taking the beer but it didn't seem to be important. I got my cigarettes off the dresser and walked over to the door.

"Johnny?"

I didn't turn around.

"You can stay if you want to, Johnny."

I found the night latch and made sure it was on.

"I had to be sure," she said softly. "I had to know if you thought enough of me to leave if I asked you."

Maybe it had taken a little persuasion to get me started but she wasn't going to have any trouble about having me stick around.

"I hope you've made up your mind," I said.

And then she was crying and talking, all at the same time, and I couldn't understand half of what she said. But I knew that she was talking about the job and how it hadn't meant anything to her, how wrong I might have been on that ten but how swell it was that I was getting myself squared away.

"I always hated that hotel," she said, trying to laugh. "The whole three years I was there."

I hadn't known she'd worked there that long.

"You've got yourself a partner," I said.

I snapped out the light, but not before I saw how she was there on the bed, all twisted up and not afraid any more. I heard my belt buckle hit the floor and I guess she heard it, too. She let out a tiny sob and then she was asking me to hurry, filling the room with the sounds of her need.

I didn't keep her waiting very long.

CHAPTER VI

Kept woman

WE MOVED into a three-room apartment on High Street, just off North. It was on the far end of town, away from the office, away from anybody I knew or anyone who might know me. It suited me fine.

"Some day," Janet said, "we'll get into a place where we can have our own furniture."

"Yeah."

"I wonder how long it'll take?"

She was sitting on the low davenport, leaning way back, her legs pushed out in front. It was hot in the apartment. She was wearing only briefs and a black net brassiere.

"I just got my license," I reminded her. "It's going to take me a while to get writing business and making some real money."

She took a deep breath and her breasts shot right up into the air. She moved her legs some, back and forth, and I moved around in the chair.

"I wish it didn't take so long," she said. She sat up suddenly, smiling. "I don't know what I'm griping about, Johnny. I'm—sort of happy. Only I wish that we could get married. It doesn't seem right, living like this."

"That's the hell of it," I said.

I got up from the chair and went over and took my coat out of the closet. It was still early in the evening, a few minutes past seven, and I didn't want to spend the whole of it batting the breeze with her. Besides, I had an appointment to sell my first life insurance policy.

"Going out, Johnny?"

"To get some of that money we need."

She laughed and came to me. I dropped the coat and got my arms around her and pulled her in close. She felt like she was naked, all warm and throbbing against me.

"Later," she whispered, moving her lips over my mouth. "Later—when there isn't any hurry."

"Okay," I said.

I didn't feel too much like leaving the house.

She didn't close the door until I was in the lower hall. Then I heard her call good-bye again and the lock clicked sharply.

The Ford coupe was parked out front. It was four years old, but in good shape and Connors had been nice enough to let me use it until I could afford one of my own.

I pointed the car cross-town, toward the corner of Main and Clarke Streets.

I felt real good.

This was my third week in the business. I'd just passed my life exam and now I was qualified to give the public a fast going over. From what I'd seen on the debit assigned to me, it was going to be better than a Sunday picnic in the country. A lot of people believe anything they're told. And I could tell them plenty.

I felt sorry as hell about Janet but there wasn't much I could do to change things. She was a good kid, a little nuts maybe, but I didn't think she was the kind of a dame I'd want to spend the rest of my life looking across a mattress at. At first, she'd been a little coy about moving in with me and if there'd have been any other answer to her problem I'd have given it to her without being asked. But she'd tried for a whole week to get a job, after the incident at the hotel, and she hadn't been able to hook one. Everybody had asked her for references and it would have taken a board of directors meeting to have gotten her one from the hotel. She hadn't said so, not in so many words, but she'd given me the feeling that I had to do something about her or that ten bucks might come up and cause me a fistful of trouble.

"We ought to be married, if we're going to live together," she'd said.

I'd had one for that, too. If I was already married I couldn't get sacked with her, not unless I got a divorce and I'd have to wait for that. I was very vague about the whole thing, telling her, and she cried because I hadn't told her about it before but she believed me and that was the important thing.

The next day we'd moved into the furnished apartment.

"It's funny I'm so scared," she'd said that night after we'd gone to bed. "I guess I hadn't ought to be scared."

"You don't have to worry," I'd said, stroking her hair. "You don't have to worry about a damned thing."

She'd kissed me long, throwing her body at me.

"Only one thing," she'd murmured. "Don't let that happen, Johnny."

"Not until we can make it right," I'd agreed.

And then she'd been mine, all mine, and she'd cried and cursed me because the night was so young and beautiful. She'd gone to sleep, her arms holding me tight, and I'd tried to think about her and how it was with us.

I was still trying to figure it out.

A girl like Janet shouldn't be shacking up with a guy like me. She ought to have more sense. But it was her business if she wanted to be so stupid. Besides, she wasn't the worst bed partner in town and I might get to like her pretty good after a while.

I parked the car on Main, just below the corner of Clarke. I rolled up the windows and locked the doors. In this part of town they'd steal the air out of your tires.

I walked back to the corner, turning left into Clarke Street. The wind was blowing damp and sharp, as it does before a thunder storm, and the assorted smells from the rendering plant, down at the end, came boiling up the street. The man who owned this stench factory was the ward alderman. I'd met him once. He'd smelled worse than his plant.

I turned in at the first house, a great, big, barn-like thing with five or six apartments clinging to the walls inside. The wooden steps protested under my weight and a dog growled from nearby.

"Johnny."

I swung away from the door, staring into the shadows.

"Hi," I said.

There was a porch swing down at the far end, one of those kind that hang from the ceiling by four chains, and she was sitting in that. Of course, it was plenty dark in there, but I was able to make out the dull white lines of her legs and the dim oval of her face.

I walked over to the swing.

"You been waiting for me?"

She nodded.

"I remembered that I didn't tell you I'd moved into a different apartment."

I sat down beside her. The swing shook on the chains and threatened to go over backward.

"I'd have found it all right," I said.

"Remember the one I used to have?"

"Top floor, left." I'd tried to get in there a couple of times but I hadn't had any luck. "One of the door panels had a hunk of plywood nailed over it."

"That's the one."

"I guess you didn't like it."

She moved around in the swing, pulling her legs up under her body. I could see the lines of her breasts, pointed and full, and I could smell the soft scent of her perfume.

"Nights during the summer," she said, "I like to sit out here on the porch, just watching. With the baby upstairs I couldn't do that. I couldn't hear the baby crying when I sat down here."

"Your mother could have called you," I said. "Or your father. They ought to be able to sit night watch for you once in a while."

"They don't live here any more, Johnny."

"Oh."

"Dad got a job on the Erie, up in Port Jervis. I've never been up there."

"You haven't missed anything," I said.

"After I had the baby—well, he'd been driving back and forth, boarding up there during the week and coming home weekends—after the baby came they decided to move. By that time I had a job, so I stayed here."

I didn't ask her any more and she didn't bother telling me. I knew it all, anyhow. She was just a girl with a kid, and she wasn't married, and her folks were sore as hell about it. Her folks ran away and she stayed, which made her about two hundred percent better than her old lady and her old man thrown together.

I got out my wallet.

"Here's that thirty I owe you," I said, handing her the ten and a twenty. "Any time you need some of the same stuff, just let me—"

"That's okay," Julie said. "I always like to see somebody from this street get a break. You didn't have to be in any hurry giving it back. There's only me and the baby and rent's cheap as dirt down here. The woman who takes the baby for me every day only charges four dollars a week."

"Just remember what I said," I told her, folding her small fingers around the money. "If you ever need any help, yell."

"Thanks, Johnny."

A life insurance man can always get his hand on a fast buck. Some people pay you their premiums way in advance, and you can play around with the money for a little while and not get caught. Like that thirty I'd just given Julie. By the time the fellow's premium was actually due I'd be able to replace it with somebody else's money, and before too long I'd be making enough on the debit so that I could square the whole thing away.

"Well," she said, getting up, "we'd better go in where there's some light."

"Okay." That was her idea, not mine. "But we don't have to be in any hurry about it."

She laughed and moved across the porch. I followed her, hearing the swish of her skirt. We went into the wide hall and she quietly opened the first door on the right.

A small table lamp burned in one corner of the room. I'd never been in this apartment before, but it looked much different than I'd expected. Instead of wide, chipped boards on the floor, there was block tile in contrasting colors of gray and blue. The walls were painted a deeper gray and the ceiling an inviting red. None of the furniture was anything to brag about, but the new slipcovers were clean and colorful.

"Not bad," I said, looking around. "You must be a first cousin of the landlord."

Or sleeping with him, I thought.

She turned on the radio and the music came on, soft and low. The light from the lamp was just enough to wash over her, bringing out the blondeness of her hair, the redness of her lips, the full, sweeping lines of her figure.

"You remember Joe Card, Johnny?"

"Yeah."

Joe had worked for the railroad and he'd got a big settlement from them when he'd lost his left arm while switching trains in the yard. He'd blown his money away on drink and clothes. At one time or another, he'd taken care of about half of the women along the street.

"This is where Joe fell and broke his neck," Julie said. "Nobody wanted the place, so I took it and fixed it up."

"All by yourself?"

She nodded.

"The tile on the floor and the painting and all that?"

"It wasn't so hard."

She sat down on the davenport, near the light, and I sat down beside her.

"I don't know how you did it."

"You get so you can do things," she said. "If you have to."

"Yeah."

We talked some more about the street, some of the people we'd known, and how lousy it could be. The program on the radio changed over to a news broadcast, and she turned it off. The night became still outside and the insects beat against the window screen. Finally we got around to why I was there, sitting beside her, and all of the nearness I'd felt for a few minutes slipped away.

"Do you think twenty payment life would be best for the baby?" she wanted to know. "Or an endowment policy?"

"If I were talking to somebody else, I'd say an endowment."

"Why?"

"There'd be more commission in it." I lit a cigarette and the smoke slid over and across her face. "But the twenty payment would do just as good and cost you a lot less."

"I think I'll take that, then. One for a thousand."

"You're doing the right thing, Julie."

I removed an application blank from my coat pocket, crossed my legs and held it on one knee.

"This is the first one I've ever filled out," I said. "I'll have to take it easy."

"I'm not rushing you."

I started asking her questions.

"What's his name?"

"Arnold."

I didn't want to ask her, but I had to.

"Arnold what?"

"Wilson," she said, tonelessly; I didn't look at her. "Just Wilson."

He was eight months old and I put that down. She said he'd never been sick so I answered no to all of the diseases. When I got to the part that asked her husband's name I just put down that she was divorced.

"Thanks," Julie said, watching as I did it.

She signed the application and I gave her a receipt for the first monthly deposit. She put the receipt in her pocketbook and I stuck the application and money in my pocket.

"Pretty damn hot," I told her. "I wish I had a beer."

"You like beer," she said. "So do I, sometimes."

It was early, the kid wasn't crying and there were just the two of us.

"I could get a couple of bottles at the corner," I said. "If you'd like."

She got up quickly, went across to the radio and turned it on again. She kicked off her shoes and started taking the bobby pins out of her hair.

"It's too late," she said. "I've got to get some sleep."

I didn't say anything. I moved over and stood behind her. Her arms were up, her hands fiddling with her hair, and I could see the jutting points of her breasts. Her back had a deep arch to it and her hips tight against the skirt. Before she knew what I was doing I put my arms around her, my hands against her flat stomach. I pressed in close and bent down and kissed her on the neck.

"What the hell's the matter with you?" I demanded. "Can't you have a beer with an old friend."

She felt around with her right foot, got her shoe on again and kicked me savagely in the shin. I let go of her. Very calmly she began to fool with her hair again.

"Next time," she said, "wait until I ask you."

"I'll be so old I won't be able to do anything about it."

"That's what I mean."

She went over to the door and held it open for me. There was a slight smile curving her lips and I had an idea that she wasn't quite as sore as she sounded.

"Goodnight," I said.

"Goodnight, Johnny."

"Thanks for the app."

"You're welcome."

I heard her close and lock the door after me. I grinned and thought about what I had missed and what I had got. I had missed her again, but there were no ground rules that said I couldn't keep trying for the jackpot. And I'd written my first life insurance application, which would put me in good at the office in the morning.

I kicked a piece of broken glass out of the way and turned left on Clarke Street. It wasn't very far down to the house and the old lady would be glad to see me.

Like hell she would.

CHAPTER VII

Home, Sweet Home

HALF-WAY DOWN the street I turned in at a dimly lighted house. Most of the windows lacked curtains and the yellow shades had ragged edges along the bottom.

This was home.

"Kill the bastard!" somebody was yelling next door. "Cut his—"

I pulled open the screen door and went inside. It was hot and dark in there but I didn't have any trouble finding the string. I started up the stairs and I noticed a lot of plaster on the steps but I didn't bother looking to see where it had come from. I looked, instead, to see if there was a light under the living room door of the downstairs apartment. There was. I decided that Lili must have had a run of good luck and that she was taking the night off—spending it alone.

I went on upstairs and into our front room. It smelled of ham and cabbage and last night's beer. I listened and pretty soon I could hear the old man snoring it off. Even without looking into the bedroom I knew just how he'd be sprawled out on top of the old brass bed. His shirt would be open, his mouth gaping wide, his false teeth somewhere on the floor. Sometimes he lost his teeth on the way home and the next day the kids would pick them up and bring his choppers back.

Once they'd been gone for a week and he'd damned near starved to death.

I went through to the kitchen. My mother stood at the sink, slowly washing some dishes, her shoulders bent far forward.

"Hi, Mom!" I said.

She swung around, looking at me, and for a couple of seconds I thought she was going to start bawling. But she didn't. She just shrugged and went back to washing dishes.

"Hello," she said.

I went over to the kitchen table and sat down.

"Where've you been?" she wanted to know after a while.

"Around," I said.

It was as hot in there as plate glass in the sun and the smells were all mixed up with it. My whole life on Clarke Street seemed to walk into the room and come showering down around me. I could see it in the chipped china on the drainboard, in the cracked and grease-stained paper on the walls, in the way my mother's bare feet spread out, wide, on the linoleum floor. I saw it all and I wanted to throw up. I'd seen and known enough of it all to last me forever.

"You been around, all right," she said, letting the water out of the sink. "Like always, you been around where nobody could find you."

"I didn't know you were looking."

"I wasn't."

"So it didn't make any difference, then."

She dried her arms with the dish towel and wiped it across her face. Her sagging breasts rose and fell against the stays of her corset. I wondered, vaguely, if she'd ever gotten a Spencer corset. She'd been yelling about one ever since I'd been a kid.

"I don't know why you don't stay home," she said. She took off her apron and gave it a heave into a corner. "It ain't natural, livin' the way you do."

"I've got a right to do what I want."

"The way you act you got plenty of rights," she said, scuffing her feet along the floor. "Look at you!"

"So what's wrong with me?"

"God, he asks what's wrong with him! Lookit the new suit, would you? And the shoes. A-ha, nothin's too good for Johnny Reagan."

"Yeah," I said. "That's me."

"You should worry about me."

"I'm worrying."

"I'd drop dead if you did. You ever worry about the rent 'round here? Only God knows how I ever pay it. And the grub. You ever do any worryin' about that? You ever worry that Sam's not here, not payin' any more?"

"Look," I said, "when I was home I paid board, didn't I? When I don't live home and I make enough dough I always send you some, don't I?"

"What's ten dollars these days?"

"Well, hell."

She kept walking around the kitchen, her bare feet making funny sounds. Her face was almost beet red and I knew that she was getting ready to burn out a bearing, or something.

"Ha!" she yelled, standing in front of me. "Lookit the suit! Just lookit him! A fancy Dan! You ever do any worryin' about anything?"

"I got four brothers," I told her. "We can leave the old man out of it. You sell them on the idea and I'll do twenty percent of all the worrying that's done around here."

"They got families." She walked back to the sink and took a drink of water. The water would be hot and taste of chemicals. "They've got themselves to think about. George's kid's been terrible sick. That costs. And Mary's expectin' again. They don't know what to do."

"They could stop having so many kids," I told her. "They must be nuts."

"I don't know what's gonna become of them."

"I'm telling you what they should do. Sleep alone."

"Maybe you're right," she admitted. "They got no sense."

"How many times am I an uncle now, huh? They multiply so fast I can't keep track of them."

She had to think that over for a minute, counting on her fingers.

"Seventeen," she said.

"They must all be hot stuff."

I got up and walked over to her. She looked so small and miserable that I bent down and kissed her. She never liked to be kissed so she wiped the spot on her cheek off with the back of one hand.

"Here's ten," I told her, sticking the bill into the pocket of her dress. "I'll send you more regular, as much as I can."

"Thanks, Johnny." Her gray eyes clouded over, like she was in pain. "I shouldn't talk that way to you, Johnny. It's only that—"

"Forget it," I said.

"You're the only one that ever put much cash in here."

"The rest of them have troubles, I guess."

"And your father's a lost cause."

"He's no great shakes," I admitted. "But he's all right, only when he drinks."

"Which is most of the time."

"Yeah."

"And he's been doin' other things, too." Her face grew suddenly hard and angry. "You know what he's been doin'?"

"I haven't any idea."

"That little bitch downstairs," she said, her lips quivering. "He's been after her, and her young enough to be his own daughter!"

"Business must be getting tough for her," I said.

"You really think she—does?"

"Hell, yes!"

She kept looking at me, breathing hard, and her eyes got cold.

"There's only one way you could know."

"Yeah," I said. "I guess that's right."

She looked hurt, like I'd slapped her. Maybe she was thinking that I'd wasted my money. She was wrong. It hadn't cost me anything.

"Don't worry about it," I told her. "He'll either stay drunk or get over it."

She didn't walk all the way out to the door with me. She hung back, telling me she wished I wouldn't go, and crinkling the ten spot.

"I'll send you some more," I said. "I'll try to make it enough."

"I won't hold my breath on it."

I told her so long and went out into the hall, closing the door after me. I went down the steps fast.

The light was still on in Lili's front room. I didn't bother knocking. If she was busy the door would be locked. If she wasn't occupied she'd like to see somebody walk in. She didn't often bring her work home with her, except for the neighbor-hood stuff, and she was pretty careful about that.

"Hello, big shot," she said lazily.

I pushed the door shut. She was stretched out on the dav-enport. The only thing she had over her was a newspaper. A small newspaper, *The Daily News*. It didn't cover much.

"Hi," I said.

"Hot, isn't it?"

"Enough."

She wasn't a big girl, not in length, but she was big in a lot of other ways. She had red-blonde hair filled with natural curls, and she kept her face in good condition. I'd heard, once, that she'd been a model someplace or other and I hadn't doubted it. She had the face and the figure and those blue eyes of hers wouldn't have had any trouble with a camera.

"Where you been keeping yourself, Johnny?"

"None of your business."

She frowned and her eyes grew dark.

"Maybe you're not welcome here, Johnny."

"Maybe."

I walked over and stood by the davenport. I tried not to look at her, except her face, but I couldn't miss the way the paper left her breasts almost bare and how it hardly covered her further down.

"You stay away from my old man," I told her.

"He won't go broke," she said. "He isn't young any more."

"I'm telling you, Lili."

"All right, you've told me."

"My old lady won't stand for it."

"A lot you care for her!"

"On this I do," I said. She was making me sore. Maybe I wasn't all a son was supposed to be, but no chippie like Lili was going to start waltzing my old man around. "Hell, there's nothing in it for you, anyway. You ought to know better than to pick on a guy like that."

She swung her legs off the davenport and got up very slowly. I watched the newspaper slide away and fall to the floor. I met her look and she knew what I'd been thinking.

"Got cheated, didn't you?"

She was wearing a very brief pair of black panties and her bra had been so far down, one of those used with strapless evening gowns, that I hadn't been able to see it.

"I wasn't paying," I said. "How could I get cheated?"

I saw her hand coming. I reached up and grabbed it, just as it whacked against my face. I brought it down alongside of me, twisting it.

"Johnny!"

I hadn't been near her in a long while and there'd only been that one time for us. I guess there could have been others but I'd never gone in much for anyone like Lili. Not that I'd thought I was any better, just because it had seemed so unnecessary.

"You staying away from the old man?" I wanted to know. I twisted her arm some more. "Say you will!"

She tried to back up but I wouldn't let her. When I put some more pressure on her arm she came up against me, breathing hard.

"Let go," she whispered, biting her lower lip. "I should get myself pulled apart for a stupid thing like this!"

"That's better."

I pushed her away from me. She walked around the room, shaking her hand, getting the blood down into her fingers.

"Well, you got what you want," she said. "Why don't you get out of here?"

"Okay."

I started over to the door but I thought of something and I stopped.

"Say," I asked her, "have you got any life insurance?"

"You'd better stay out of the sun, Johnny."

"Don't get wise, Lili. You know what I mean. You pay a half a buck a week and you get a policy that pays off when you die."

"Well, that's great," she said. She went back to the davenport and sat down. Her face was flushed and the rest of her body had taken on a new glow. She didn't look bad at all. "That's the best I've heard today. I work all my life and somebody else picks up the loot after they plant me. To hell with that."

"I wasn't thinking of that so much," I told her, "Any life insurance pays off when you die, but I was thinking of a policy that you could collect in money, yourself, someday."

"Maybe I should have an accident policy," she said, tossing her head back and laughing. "If you know what I mean."

I told her that I knew but that I didn't have one and it wouldn't be any good to her if I did. I kept talking about how she ought to save some money, what an endowment contract could do for her, and it wasn't long before I was over on the davenport with her. She kept her eyes closed, listening, and she didn't open them when I kissed her.

"You ought to do all right in the insurance business," she said.

I had an application in my pocket and I got that out. She answered all the questions I asked her and when I got to the part about her occupation she said she was an entertainer.

"I could show you," she said.

I asked her the rest of the questions, the medicals and the other stuff, and she signed the app without bothering to look it over.

I got up and walked to the door.

"When the policy comes through I'll give it to the agent on this debit and you can pay him."

"What's he like? A nice fellow?"

"Sure."

Her eyes looked dreamy and she smiled. She was going to get fooled. The guy who worked Clarke Street was in his seventies.

I told her goodnight and went out, feeling good. It was my first day selling and I had two apps.

One bastard.

And one joy girl.

Nothing but the best.

CHAPTER VIII

Business before Pleasure

IT TOOK ME almost three months to get my feet out of the mud. There's a lot of angles to being a life insurance salesman and you either learn them or you get tossed out of the business.

"Nice sale," Connors would tell me.

"Thanks."

He never asked if I lied or told the truth or anything like that. When it got to my turn I'd drift into his big office and put my report down on the top of his desk. He saw the industrial applications I wrote, the nickel-to-a-dollar-a-week kind, and he saw the fives and the tens and the twenties in the ordinary department. He liked those ordinary applications because ten or twenty thousand dollars of life insurance protection meant a fast buck for him. Not that he needed the money. He had so much coming in all the time and he was so lousy with success that he should have had somebody scratching his back for him.

"I'll return your car in the morning," I told him one day. "I got hold of a Ford that looks pretty good."

"You didn't have to do that, Johnny."

"I feel like a fool, running around in your car all the time."

"You shouldn't, Johnny."

"I'd hate to tell that to the other agents."

He laughed and lit a cigar. He'd been real decent to me, right along, asking me out to the lake during the summer to swim and for supper under the pines once in a while. Of course the other agents in the office didn't go for that as much as I did, but that was their own fault. Some of them were so damned lazy they wouldn't even look at a clock to find out the right time of the day. A couple had been in the business for over twenty years, all of it with Connors, but most of the others were just passing through, earning a living while they scouted around for something else.

"This is Friday," Connors told me.

No insurance man has to be told when it's Friday. That's pay day, the end of the week, the day when a guy can go out and get drunk and try to make somebody else's wife.

"Like to have you out for dinner tonight, Johnny."

I hadn't been out there for over ten days but I knew that Janet would raise hell about it. I'd been working late almost every night, selling insurance, and we hadn't gone any place. I'd promised her, though, that this weekend we'd take a run up into the mountains, rent a room, get loaded and try to figure out where we were going.

"Thanks," I said to Connors. "But I've got something on for tonight and I'll have to ask for a rain-check."

Anytime I was stupid enough to ask for a rain-check to sit across from his pinched-face wife I ought to have my skull examined.

"There won't be many nice days left," Connors said. He got up and went over to the window; the September sun blazed warm on the red and gray carpet. "I thought it might be the last chance for the Missus and Beverly and the two of us to sit out under the pines."

That was sure a hell of a way to spend an evening. The mosquitoes always buzzed around under the pines, sucking more blood out of my arms than I had in my whole body. If his daughter had been somebody like Julie Wilson I'd have gone out there if I had to walk through the woods barefooted. But Beverly left me cold; she left me so cold that every time I looked at her I thought winter had set in.

"We get some nice weather in October," I said. "Sometimes it's hotter in October than it is right now."

He puffed thoughtfully on his cigar and the blue spirals of smoke crawled upwards through the sunlight.

"I'm not going to be here in October," he said.

I shrugged and picked up my report off the desk. I couldn't see what he was so annoyed about but I didn't want to get into it any further with him. I liked Connors and I liked his job but all the rest of it I could skip and not ever miss.

"Maybe we could make it next week," I said.

Next week, in two weeks, almost any time but this night. Somehow I had to get a few hours with Janet and fix things with her. I'd told her so much about the girl I was trying to get loose from, to keep her away from Connors, that I couldn't even get it straight myself. On top of that, she'd come up with the idea that she was pregnant and that she was going to have a kid almost any day. She had me running around like a fly on a piece of bread.

"Whatever it is," Connors said, "you'll have to put it off, Johnny. I've got something on my mind and I want to talk it over with you. It's about my going away in October."

"I don't know where you could go," I said.

He pushed up the window and pitched the cigar outside. He was always throwing things out of the window. I wondered that the city put up with it.

"It's like this, Johnny," he said. He went back to the desk and sat down. He put another cigar in his mouth and chewed on it. "The old lady and I've wanted to take a long trip for so damn many years I can't remember."

"You should get a trailer."

He shook his head.

"Where we're going a trailer wouldn't be any good. We've talked a lot about traveling in Europe—not just one country, or two countries, but every last one of them."

"I see."

He struck a match and tried to get the cigar going but he'd chewed it so much that it wouldn't work. He swore and threw the cigar in the waste can. That guy spent enough on cigars to support a family of five.

"We've been talking about it again lately," he said. "We've been planning about really doing it at last. Do you know why?"

"Why?"

"Because I think you can run this place for me while I'm gone, Johnny."

I slowly put my report down on his desk. I stuck my hands in my pockets and leaned back on my heels, staring down into his fat face. I felt like asking him if he was blowing a spoke out of one of his wheels. He'd been nice to me and all that and I'd been doing a good job, but I hadn't expected anything quite so big.

"I hope you know what you're saying, Mr. Connors."

He grinned and rocked around in his swivel chair.

"You can bet on that, Johnny."

I was pretty sure that he didn't know but I wasn't going to argue with him about it.

"That's what I wanted to talk to you about," he said. "There's a couple of more things that I have to iron out before we discuss it in detail, but they'll be squared away by tonight."

"I see."

He gave me a big grin and tapped his fingernails on the top of the desk.

"I think you'd be making a big mistake to turn down my invitation, Johnny."

"I guess I would."

"So I'll expect you?"

I wondered about Janet and how she'd scream at me. She'd told me a lot of times that if I didn't treat her right she was going to phone Connors and tell him what I'd done at the hotel and how I was living with her and a lot of other things.

She could go to hell.

"Okay," I said. "I'll be there."

"Bring your swimsuit. You and Beverly can have another race."

"Okay."

We'd done that a few times, in the early dark of evening, racing each other out to the float about two hundred feet off shore. I'd always beaten her easily and I'd be sitting on the float, laughing at her, when she got there. One night she'd been very tired and I'd had to help pull her up on the planks. The moon had been out high and bright and the top of her suit had dropped down. For just a couple of seconds her breasts had been right there in front of me, firm and round and white. It'd been the only time that she'd interested me in the least but I hadn't done anything about it. Bothering her, I figured, would be worse than starting a forest fire in a high wind.

"Send Sammy Grick in, Johnny."

"Sure."

I waved at Connors and went out to the agents' room. The place looked like a country school house, with short rows of lift-up top desks, hard cane chairs and a blackboard at one end.

"Hey, Sammy," I said. "The old man wants a pint of your blood."

Sammy got up, kicking the chair away from his desk, Sammy Grick was a skinny kid, around twenty-five, with a hungry face and huge black eyes. He always walked with a slight stoop, as though the wind was blowing at his back, and he made it his business not to smile more than once a day.

"I'll give him a whole quart," Sammy said. "I got a ten last night."

Sammy was the only competition I had in the office. Abe Wulderstein's father had left him a pot full of money and he was in the business for kicks. Jack Carter was going on sixty and he had arthritis in his knees so bad that he'd rather hang himself than climb a pair of stairs. Willie Dixon was shopping around for a job where it would only be necessary for him to continue breathing in order to make a living, and Roy Johnson was so old that he couldn't see good, even with thick glasses, and he kept getting the rates all screwed up.

"So long, slaves," I told them and went through to the waiting room.

Most of the morning they'd sit there and gripe, why they hadn't made this or that sale and why this bastard or that bastard wouldn't pay his premium on time. They didn't know what it was all about. They were camping out in a field of clover and they couldn't see it for the weeds.

I went up to the cashier's window.

"Hi," Julie Wilson said.

She got up from her typewriter and straightened her skirt. She had on a gray thing that hung on her hips like a snake's skin and her red blouse was all bumps and movement as she came up to the window.

"Big week," she said and gave me my check.

I looked at it; a hundred and six dollars after deductions.

"Slow," I said.

She put her elbows on the counter, held her chin in her hands and stared at me.

"You're a real clown," she said.

"Thanks."

"But I'm proud of you," she said seriously. "I'm really proud of somebody who came up from Clarke Street and made good."

I thought about what Connors had just told me in his office. She didn't know how good I was doing. I was on the verge of doing so good that I was almost scared.

"Yeah," I said.

She stood up, stretching, and the front of her red blouse climbed right up in the air.

"I got a new Ford that's the nuts," I told her. "How about Sunday at two?"

I'd seen her a couple of Sundays and we'd gone down to the river swimming. I hadn't had any luck, so this time I thought maybe we could drive out to some inn, find a nice quiet corner and break out a jug. Of course, I didn't have much time even on Sundays, because Janet didn't go for the long excuses and I had to keep thinking fast all the while. But I wasn't worrying about Janet right then. I had something else on my mind.

"Gee, I can't," Julie said. "Not Sunday."

"You should get out and relax on a weekend."

"That's what I'm going to do, Johnny."

"Yeah?"

She tossed her blonde hair and gave me a wet smile that would have floored two men.

"At last I got myself a boyfriend," she said, "An honest-to-God gentleman boyfriend."

I looked her body over carefully.

"That hadn't ought to be hard to do," I said.

"He works on the gas line."

"Must be from Oklahoma."

"Texas," she said. "His name's Billy Duke."

"Hell of a name."

"They all call him Dooder."

"That's even worse."

We talked some more about it. She said that the gas line would soon be strung across the mountains and that this guy would be moving on. She'd only been out with him three times and already he wanted to marry her and show her how to ride horses in Texas and all that junk. I got the impression that she wasn't so much in love with him as she was glad to find somebody she could talk to and who didn't know more about her business than she did.

"Of course he doesn't know about the baby yet," she said. "That might spoil it."

"Yeah," I agreed, "it might."

I took the elevator down to the street level and went outside. The sun was clear and hot and the shade from the awning out front felt good. The five-and-ten had the beach balls out again and some kid was screaming at his mother because she was too tight to buy one.

I went across the street and got into the Ford. It was a forty-nine, but it was in good shape and the red paint job looked like new. The fellow who'd owned it had put on a duel exhaust system and it snarled like a piece of cloth ripping on barbed wire when I shot it out into the traffic.

I drove over to the apartment.

It was hot in there, even with the windows wide open, and I could hear the water drumming in the shower.

The sound of the water died to a whisper.

"That you, Johnny?"

I gave her a big laugh.

"Expecting somebody else?"

She gave me a laugh in return.

"You know better than that, Johnny."

"Sure."

She was a good kid and I had to lie to her and I didn't give a damn.

"About that trip," I told her. "We've got to break it off for this weekend."

I'd given it to her quick, right off the shoulder, and I expected her to yell at me. She didn't.

"That's good," she said. "Hand me a towel, Johnny."

I went to the closet and got a rough white towel off a shelf. I pulled the shower curtain aside and I saw her standing naked and wet in there. She took the towel and wrapped it around her tight little breasts and flat middle.

"Be a hon, Johnny, and get me my robe."

I went out to the bedroom and pulled the robe out of the two-by-one hole in the wall. When I got back to the bathroom she turned her back to me, let the towel drop, and I slid the robe onto her.

"Gosh, baby," I said, "I didn't mean to give you the business this weekend, but—"

"I said it was good, didn't I?"

"I know, but you were so high about it the other night when I suggested it," I said. She still had her back to me and I put my arms around her, feeling her flat tummy. She leaned her head back and her hair felt wet against my shoulder. "You really don't care, do you?"

"No, Johnny."

"That's funny."

"Is it?"

She reached down and worked my hands loose. Then she turned around, slowly, until she stood there facing me. A tiny smile puckered the corners of her mouth and she blinked her eyes furiously.

"A lot of things are funny," she said.

"Yeah."

"You and me, Johnny—right from the start."

"I'm not laughing, baby."

I thought about the other night and how she'd cried in bed and how the prospects of her having a kid had froze me fast to the sheets. If she was going to laugh about that now I was going to get plenty sore at her.

"I found myself a job today," she said.

"You don't have to work."

She shook her head.

"I want to work, Johnny." She looked away and down. "I want to get back something that I've lost."

"Okay, but you won't find it working."

"And I got myself a room," she said, ignoring me. She tried to laugh but it broke off and fell away. "It's right near the lunchroom. All I have to do is fall out of bed and I'm on the job."

"Well, suit yourself," I told her. If she thought I was going to ask her to stay she'd made a left turn on a busy street. "You ought to know what you're doing."

For just a moment she looked up at me, her mouth hurt and her eyes deep and dark. And, then, she was up tight, her fingers digging into my flesh, and she was telling me how it was with her and why it wasn't any good for us.

"I was so scared!" she breathed. "When you were sound asleep I'd sit up in bed and cry—it was so awful. I kept feeling the baby inside of me, getting bigger, and I hated you and I wished that I'd die. But when I found out that I was wrong, that there wouldn't be any baby and I didn't have to be afraid of that, I didn't hate you any more. I tried to hate you and I couldn't—and it frightened me."

I didn't bother telling her so but she'd just pulled a two ton weight off of what was left of my nerves.

"Listen!" I said. "Don't cry any more, baby."

"Even after I called the office yesterday, I couldn't hate you," she went on. "I asked how I could get in touch with your wife and they said you were single and that you didn't have any wife. I cried about that all afternoon."

"You shouldn't do so much crying," I told her. "I was only trying to get set with some money before we jumped off the cliff."

"It wouldn't have cost any more to have lived married than it's cost us this way."

I didn't bother answering her.

"You know that, Johnny, don't you?"

I shrugged and pulled myself loose. I walked over to the mirror and looked at my face. I'd have to shave before I went out to Connors.

"When are you shoving off?" I asked her.

She bit her lower lip and stared at the floor.

"Right now. As soon as I get dressed."

"No hard feelings?"

Her laugh was bitter.

"You needn't worry," she said. "I won't say anything to Mr. Connors about what happened at the hotel and I won't cause you any trouble."

"Thanks."

"I—I love you, Johnny. That makes a difference."

She walked over to pick up the towel and the robe dipped apart in the middle. When she straightened up the robe split wide open and all I could see was her white body and her dark hair and her parted red lips.

"Baby," I said.

After she'd told me about the kid, I'd been scared and timid and I hadn't bothered her at all. But now she was all right and she was a woman and I was a man and we were all alone.

"Johnny!"

I ripped the towel out of her hands and tossed it over my shoulder.

"Please don't, Johnny!"

I turned her around and pulled the robe down off her shoulders. It got tangled up in my feet but I kicked it loose and

I picked her up. The hollows of her knees were warm against my hand.

"I'm still leaving you, Johnny."

"All right."

I carried her into the bedroom. "Be careful, won't you?" she begged as I put her down on the bed.

"Sure."

I closed the Venetian blinds and banged the door shut. The blue walls of the room became a murky gray. I watched her as I got out of my clothes. She lay there on the bed, not moving, her body full and alive and relaxed.

"I ought to hate you," she said as I lay down beside her.

"But you don't."

I drew her close and her lips brushed against my mouth.

"But I don't," she repeated.

She cried and moaned a little as I found and knew her again. She bit my lip, low on the inside, and some of the blood got on her and she didn't mind a bit. She swore at me and she told me I was no good and she loved me all the way.

I was five minutes late getting out to Connors' place but I was able to explain that pretty easily. I just told him that I'd been real busy.

CHAPTER IX

The Big Wheel

CONNORS and his wife sailed from New York the following Saturday. After the boat wandered off down river Beverly and I went back to the car and I drove her home. I now had the apartment to myself, so I spent the weekend in there sleeping and thinking and drinking. Monday morning I went over to the office and fired Moss Collins.

"My God, Johnny!" he said, pushing his chin down into his chest. "You can't do this to me!"

We were in my office—Connors' office—and I was sitting there behind that great big desk looking across at him. He was a tired little man, about sixty, and the wrinkles in his face were all pulled out of shape.

"I'm doing it," I said.

He jerked up his head and put his hands on the desk. He leaned across it, toward me, his brown eyes steady and wet.

"I've always done my job here, Johnny."

"Sure."

"Mr. Connors wouldn't let you do this, Johnny. If he were here, he wouldn't let you do it. I've worked twenty years for him, night and day. Sometimes, at the start, he couldn't pay me every week and I worked just the same."

"I'm telling you how it is, Moss."

The tears crowded out of his eyes and sparkled on his pale cheeks.

"Tell me what's wrong, Johnny."

I stood up.

"You're a damn crook," I told him.

He backed up like I'd whacked him one across the face. I went around the desk and took him by the elbow and opened the door. I pushed him out into the office and over to the cashier's box.

"Count that money," I told him.

His hands shook as he pulled the big box open and stared down at the tray of money. A white slip of paper lay in one of the sections on top of some twenties.

"What's that paper say, Moss?"

"Eight hundred and ninety dollars and forty cents."

"Yeah. And that much is supposed to be in there?"

"That's right, Johnny."

"Then count it."

"All right," he said. "I'll count it, Johnny."

While he was doing that I wandered around the office. It was pretty crowded back there with machines and files and that sort of stuff.

The nose and the glasses I'd met on my first visit to the Connors Agency belonged to Stella Fisher. She'd spoken to me twice—that first day and the day Connors told everybody I was top dog.

"Hello, Stella," I said.

She sat at a small desk deep in one corner, her back to everybody, her mind just about as blank as the wall itself.

"Why, Mr. Reagan!"

Her eyes rolled around behind the glasses. She pushed some of the stringy hair out of her face and tried to smile.

"I wanted to talk to you," I said.

"Yes?"

"Hell, I don't even know what you do around here," I said.

She eased her chair back and stood up. She was a short woman with slightly hunched shoulders on the frame of a skeleton. She always wore black, making herself look like something that was ready to crawl into a six-foot hole.

"I answer the phone sometimes," she said.

I knew that. And she wasn't any good at it. Her telephone voice was even worse than her face.

"Go on."

"And I do some typing."

"All right."

"And the daily record, Mr. Reagan." Her face brightened. "I keep a daily record of everything that goes on. I've been doing that ever since I worked for Mr. Connors. It's sort of a—diary."

"It's a waste of time," I said. "We won't do that any more."

"But, Mr. Reagan, I—"

"There won't be any discussion about it," I said. "That junk is out. From now on we're *working* in this office, doing business. No more part-time writing jobs and goofing off. This is a business office and that's the way we're going to run it."

"I see."

"But you don't see, Stella. I'm trying to give it to you slow and easy. I'm trying to tell you that you don't have a job any more. Not after today. I'm giving you two weeks pay and that's the end of it."

Pain pulled at her lips and then rode up into her eyes. She started to tremble and I thought she was going to drop as though I'd slugged her with a club.

"I don't know," she said. "I don't know."

"You'll get something else."

Her lips curled away from her teeth.

"Of course, Mr. Reagan."

"If there's anything I can do—"

She nodded.

"You can do something. You can tell me how I can take care of my sick sister when I don't have any work. You can tell me how I can get an office job at sixty. You can tell me those things, Mr. Reagan." Her voice rose sharply. "Can you tell me, Mr. Reagan? Can you!"

"No," I said, turning away. "Figure them out for yourself."

I walked off and left her. I heard her sit down and I heard her start to cry. A thing like that wasn't good for the office but it'd be over with pretty soon and she'd be on her way. She could sit home and keep her own diary. She wasn't going to hang around me and put down on paper, for Connors to read, all of the things I had in mind doing. He might read it. And he might not like it.

"Hi, Skippy!"

"Hi, Johnny!"

The girl who took care of the overdue premiums, typing reminders to policy-holders, was short and overstocked with bulges. She had thick legs and wide, uneven teeth. I guess she liked to be called Skippy because maybe it put her in mind of being small and light and full of hell. Her boyfriend called her Skippy and every time he got home from his job on a ship, for a few days, she wasn't worth a damn for a week afterward.

They said that she didn't sleep while he was home and that she didn't sleep after he'd gone, either, because she kept thinking about it so much.

"What's Stella crying for?"

"She got the boot."

"Well, you won't see me crying."

"Or me."

"She's just an old bag."

The inside office was laid out in sort of an L shape and I went around that. Three more girls worked back there. Cindy Bartlet, a flashy little redhead who was married to some shoe clerk, took care of checking over the agents' accounts. She had a nice smile and they didn't argue with her very much.

"Doing all right, Cindy?"

"Okay, Johnny."

"Let me know if those guys give you a hard time."

"I'm watching the boss," she said.

I laughed.

"Bring your husband around to the party Friday night," I said. "Tell him he can get crocked."

"What party?"

"Right here. On me. Nothing to eat and plenty to drink."

"Sure, Johnny. We'll bring a pail and take some home."

"Bring a barrel."

I went on by and said hello to Ester Denning. Ester checked new policies and raised hell with the home office and tried to get the agents what they wanted. Ester was around forty but she used plenty of paint and wore enough support for half a dozen women. She always gave me the impression that she'd be willing to sleep with anybody who'd stay awake half the night.

"That party goes for you, too," I told her.

"You couldn't keep me away."

"You have any preference?"

She glanced up from a policy she was checking and smiled.

"Men? Or drinks?"

I gave her a big grin.

"Drinks, of course."

She sighed and leafed through the policy.

"Anything I can swallow," she said.

I gave her a pat on the back, feeling the strap of her bras-siere, and swung away.

"I'll be there," she said.

I started across to Julie's desk and then I stopped. Her chair was as empty as the day it had left the factory. A gray line of smoke crept up from a cigarette that had burned short and toppled off the ash tray onto the top of the desk. I went over and stubbed the cigarette out, getting the ends of my fingers black.

"Thanks, Johnny. Careless of me."

"Yeah."

I could smell her perfume but when I turned around I stopped smelling.

She had on a pale yellow skirt that matched her hair and she was wearing a purple sweater. The sweater had narrow, yellow half moons in it that came up and met in a V shape between her pointed breasts. I had all I could do to stop from putting my hands where they hadn't ought to go.

"You're going to drive the agents nuts," I told her. "You're going to get them so they won't work at all."

"Always cracking off, aren't you?"

I shrugged and lit a cigarette. A typewriter clicked around the corner of the L and out on the street a couple of car horns fought a fast duel.

"Why don't you tell Stella some of your jokes?" Julie demanded, going around her desk. "Get her to laugh some, Johnny. She's crying her heart out."

"She'll get over it."

"You get over dying, too, Johnny."

I circled the desk and came up beside her. She picked up some papers and shuffled them around.

"Moss is crying, too," she said. "It's an awful thing to see a man cry."

I'd seen men cry plenty of times—at the tracks because they'd lost money, at a bar because they'd lost a woman, on a park bench because they didn't have anything to lose.

"Yeah," I said. "It's a jerky thing to do."

She held the papers tight in her fist for a second and then she yanked a drawer open and slammed them inside. She got up, pushing past me, and went over to the window. I followed her, wondering why she should get so sore.

"Look," I said, but she wouldn't look. I put my hand on her shoulder and she edged away. "Look, Julie, I'm only doing these things to try to make this a better organization."

"I didn't know you were a crusader."

"And none of this affects you—none of it. You've got the same job and you're going to get more money and you haven't a thing to worry about."

"What do you think Mr. Connors is going to say about all this?"

"That's my business, Julie. That doesn't concern anybody else."

By the time Connors got back and started doing any real thinking he'd only be wasting his time.

"You think he's going to blow a tire off of his wheel just because I canned somebody who wasn't doing hardly anything?"

She thought about that for a moment.

"Come to think of it, Johnny, Stella's job never did make sense. She was supposed to break me in when I started here and she hardly knew what it was all about."

"See what I mean?"

"But Moss Collins—gee, Johnny, he's working all the time, trying to keep things—"

"He's a crook," I said.

She pulled herself around, her eyes blazing.

"That's a damn lie! He's just an old man and you're stepping all over him!"

I liked the way she looked when she was mad, her face flushed and her lips trembling slightly.

"Okay," I said. "I'll show you."

She was the only person in the office I had to prove anything to. She'd known me down there on Clarke Street, how I used to swipe apples off the corner fruit stand and lift the change out of the milk bottles over on Willard Street. They were little things, maybe, but there had been some others, too—the time I was booted out of the Methodist Sunday School because I'd used the class funds to get myself a new bike. And the time the cops had yanked me down to the station because some chippie claimed I'd rolled her for fifty bucks after she'd left her man. They weren't much, just enough for her to remember. And I didn't want her to think about them too much. If she thought about them she might get some ideas about my plans for the Connors Insurance Agency, and then I'd have to get rid of her. I didn't want to get rid of her. She had something that I wanted.

I went around the L and right over to Moss Collins. He stood there by the money, looking down at it.

"How'd it come out?" I asked

He shook his head, saying nothing.

"Answer me."

"It was short," he said listlessly. "Almost two hundred short."

"Okay," I said. "Get your coat and beat it."

"But what about the—shortage?"

"You won't get your two weeks' pay," I told him. "Now, beat it before I get the bonding company on your back."

He turned away, stumbling toward the door. I didn't even watch him go. I was looking at Julie's face, finding fifty percent of what I wanted. But the fifty percent she wouldn't give me was the kind of stuff you get on back roads after dark.

I went inside my private office and closed the door. I'd only been in there a couple of seconds when the buzzer under the desk snarled like a cat with a broken leg. I picked up the phone.

"Reagan speaking."

"That's not very businesslike, Johnny."

"Oh, hello, Beverly."

"You ought to say Mr. Reagan."

"Okay."

I guess she thought she had a nice laugh on the phone because she did it all the time. She sounded like a dull saw going through a wet plank. It was just one of those things that I had to endure, simply because Connors had been stupid enough to have slept one night too many with her mother.

"Things going pretty good, Johnny?"

"Not bad. I've been on a firing jag this morning."

"Who got it?"

I told her. It seemed better for her to get it straight from the horse's mouth.

"I'm glad I don't know anything about the business," she said. "I can't even get interested in it."

"I was just telling you, that's all."

She laughed some more and I laid the phone down on the desk until she stopped.

"I'm lonely as hell, Johnny," she said. "Why don't you run out for dinner tonight and cheer me up?"

That was one sure way of wasting an evening.

"I ought to do some work," I said.

"You don't have to stay long. I'll have steaks and we can cook them over the fireplace. I'm closing up the cabin tomorrow and moving back to town. We won't have another chance."

That was tough.

"I really ought to work," I insisted.

I didn't have a thing to do. If I could arrange it, I might call on Janet and get in some exercise.

"I wish you would," she said.

She was the boss's daughter and she could cause me plenty of trouble if she made up her mind to it. Janet didn't finish work until nine and sometimes she got stuck for a while after that. It seemed rather silly to argue with Beverly about such a minor thing,

"Okay," I said. "I'll be out around seven."

"Bring your cook book."

"Yeah."

I hung up and went around the desk and sat down. I made a complete circle in the old swivel chair but the thing wouldn't squeak the way it would for Connors. I grinned. Pretty soon it would screech so much I wouldn't be able to stand it. I'd take up where he'd left off.

Sammy Grick called about noon and wanted to know if he could have the afternoon off. He said he had a gut ache and that he wanted to lay down for a while. I laughed and told him to get up and take off before her old man got home. He said he would.

I went out for lunch at one and came back around two. There was a note on my desk to call operator 4 in New York. I put in the call and hung around waiting for it to come through.

It was the agency supervisor of The Provider Insurance Company. Yes, he'd received my letter and everybody down there was real hot about the Connors Agency taking on a franchise. They'd looked up the agency and they'd found out it was big, with plenty of power behind it. Did we have a local radio station? Hell, yes, we had one that blabbed all day long. That was fine, just fine, because we were in a lush area and this was great stuff to sell over the air.

"Somebody'll be up to see you in a few days," he said. "Maybe the boss'll be up."

"Okay."

"We ought to be able to do some business, Reagan."

"That's why I wrote."

"And that's why I called."

We said good-bye and I hung up. I lit a cigarette and walked around the office. Finally I stopped walking and stood looking down at the street. Some people mooched about in the sun, pushing baby carriages, carrying groceries. I grinned. They didn't know what it was all about.

I knew a little bit about The Provider Insurance Company. They were licensed in New York State and that's why I'd gone after them. They had a real trick policy, one for sickness and accident, the kind that gives the sucker all the protection he needs on the first page—and then uses up the next seven pages quoting clauses that take the benefits away from him.

I went over to the cabinet, where I'd hidden the bottle, and had a drink. To luck. To screwing the public. To Johnny Reagan.

I went out and wandered through the office, came back inside and did some work until four. When I had it figured out how I could make twenty-five grand a year I stopped working. I tried to call Janet but remembered Monday was her day off at the place and she didn't have a phone at her home. I thought maybe I ought to call Beverly and tell her I couldn't make it but I changed my mind about that. I never got over to Janet's before nine, anyway, and, besides, I ought to start breaking off with that. She was scared all the time and sometimes she cried because she was afraid our luck would run out. Once in a while I got the creepy feeling that she cried because she couldn't get herself fixed up real good.

I had two more drinks.

Everybody went home at five but I waited until five-thirty before I went out there and opened the cash box with the key Connors had left me. I took two hundred dollars out of my wallet and dropped the bills inside. Then I locked the box and put the key in my pocket.

Things were working out pretty good.

CHAPTER X

Seduction

I GOT OUT to Willow Lake around seven. The Connors cabin was the only place where there were lights. The other shacks were closed up, some just until hunting season—that would be the later part of October and most of November—and the rest until the next spring.

I parked the car in the drive and walked through the shadows to the porch. She pulled the door open and the light from a big blaze in the fireplace fell outside.

"You're on time, Johnny."

"Never find me late for steak."

Or any kind of meat, I thought, looking at her. She had on a black dress, cut real low, and she had a tiny watch pinned over her left breast. I knew what time it was, all right. It was time to stop looking.

"I didn't fix anything yet," she said. "Come on in."

It was hot in there and I took my coat off right away.

"Drink?"

I hung my coat over a chair.

"Sure."

She brought me beer because she knew I liked beer. She had a shot of something or other and a glass of plain water.

She spilled some of the drink across her hand and I got the impression that she'd been hitting it up just a little.

"Loneliest, stinking damned place in the world," she said.

I knew, then, that she was feeling a trifle high. She walked across the room, weaving carelessly, and slumped down on the davenport.

"First time I ever heard you say anything like that," I told her.

"First time Mother hasn't been around to guard her precious daughter."

"Maybe that's it."

"They wanted me to go with them." She held up the drink, staring at it. "Isn't that a laugh? I should go with them so I could get to bed at ten every night and watch the sun come up in the morning."

I didn't say anything. I looked around the fireplace but I couldn't see where she'd started to fix anything.

"Another drink, Johnny?"

"Okay."

I poured them this time, mixing hers with the water and keeping it as weak as possible. I didn't want her getting gassed and crying on my shoulder half the night.

"I like it better here, anyway," she said.

"I thought you were moving in to town tomorrow."

"I might change my mind."

I sat down in a chair, facing her. She set the drink on the floor and leaned back, closing her eyes. Her knees parted for a second and I stopped watching her face.

"There's something I wanted to tell you," she said slowly. "I'm glad you could come out."

"All right."

She sat up again, straightening her skirt. Then she leaned forward with the light from the fire slashing her across the face. She looked like a second edition of her old lady.

"I haven't seen you since your promotion," she said. "Except the day you brought me back from New York and I forgot about it then. Congratulations, Johnny!"

"Thanks."

"For one solid year you're going to be a great big wheel."

"I don't get it, Beverly."

"That's how long they'll be gone."

"I didn't know that," I said. "I figured on six months."

She smiled and picked up her drink.

"You ought to feel better," she said, across the glass, "now that you know."

I finished the beer but it might as well have been water. My mind was going around like a squirrel on a wheel. She'd always acted all right before but now I could feel her sticking the needle in and probing around. Maybe it was because the old man liked me and he kept talking to her about it and she got sore at him for thinking some other people were alive in the world.

"Mr. Collins was out here this afternoon," she said. She looked at me straight, her eyes black and deep. "You're a louse, Johnny."

"He's a crook."

"Everybody's entitled to a mistake."

"Not that kind."

She finished her drink in silence. I kept thinking of all of the things I could say to her and all the things I shouldn't say. I just kept my mouth shut

"Maybe you're right," she admitted, standing up. The black dress pulled in tight around her body, rolling up into a tiny bunch above her hips. "Well, what's the use of arguing about it?"

"I don't know. Is that what you wanted to tell me?"

I followed her movements as she went over and stood in front of the fireplace.

"No," she said. "That isn't what I wanted to tell you, Johnny."

"What, then?"

The flames roared through a dry piece of chestnut wood and a couple of embers shot out onto the stone hearth.

"You're a pretty big guy in my father's book, Johnny."

"He's given me a nice break," I said.

She turned around with the fire to her back. I could see the shadows of her legs against the red coals. Her throat was long and white and her face looked flushed with something other than the drinks or the heat in the room.

"Don't hurt him," she said. "Don't ever do that, Johnny."

I knew how it must have been for her that afternoon with Moss coming around and her thinking about things. Maybe she'd taken a couple of fast ones so she could think better, only they'd mixed her up all the more.

"You don't have to worry about that," I said. "You can put that one in mothballs, Beverly."

I went across and stood in front of her, my eyes not telling her anything about what was going on inside. She was just a young kid who had her nose in somebody else's business.

"Your dad won't know his agency when he gets back," I told her. If I had my way nobody else would know it either.

"I'm sorry," she said. "I shouldn't have drunk anything and I shouldn't have talked that way to you. I had no reason to say it, Johnny."

Maybe she didn't know what it was, but she had a reason all right. She was upper class and I was sitting at the bottom of the stairs looking up at her. We both knew it—only I knew what it meant and she didn't. It meant that she distrusted me because she didn't understand why I should be there. It meant that I had to keep her in line or she'd cut the horses away from my wagon and I'd find myself going downhill in reverse.

"What happened to the steak?" She was real close and I could see the points of her breasts jut up and out as she breathed. Her stomach was flat, hardly any at all, and her hips were rounded and full. She was ninety-nine percent woman. The other one percent belonged to her head.

"There isn't any steak."

"You're a hell of a hostess."

"I guess I just wanted to talk."

"We might just as well keep on drinking while we do that."

She swung away and the bottom of her dress swirled up around her knees. She started to pour the drinks but then she stopped and stood staring out of the window.

"God, it's a lovely night!"

"Yeah."

"Not cold, is it?"

"No."

"We ought to go for a swim."

"What!"

She faced me, laughing. My eyes moved away from her face and down over her body.

"The water ought to be warm."

"I didn't bring my suit," I said.

"You could wear your shorts. It isn't as though it were daylight."

I really didn't want to go in, but the water might sober her up and I didn't feel like squabbling with her.

"Okay," I said.

She walked toward the door.

"I haven't got any suit either," she said. "So you know what I'm going to do."

We went outside and down the path, in the direction of the lake. I held her arm and she leaned up close once or twice but I didn't do anything about it.

"I'll meet you out at the raft," she said.

She cut through the shadows along the shoreline and pretty soon she was out of sight. I could hear her walking through the dry leaves on the sand but after a while that stopped.

I took off my clothes and put them in a pile. I took off the shorts, too. I couldn't see any sense getting them wet and sitting around half the night while they dried in front of the fireplace. Besides, it was dark as the inside of a room out there and what she couldn't see wouldn't scare her.

I walked down to the edge of the water and stepped in. I didn't have any trouble getting wet. I'd stepped off into six feet of water.

I came up, swearing, and she laughed at me out of the darkness. I pushed the hair out of my eyes and started cutting through the water in the direction of the raft. I went past it once and I had to come back, but before she got into the water I was sitting up there on the planks, waiting for her.

"Where are you, Johnny?"

"Right here."

"My, it's dark!"

"Yeah."

"Keep calling me so I can find it."

I began to whistle and she swam toward me. She had nice clean strokes and she hardly made any noise at all. She was beside the raft almost before I knew it.

"Help me up."

I stood up and reached down for her hands. It was a good thing that it was dark because if she had seen me then she'd have drowned herself right there in the middle of the lake.

"Air's cold," she said.

"Yeah."

We sat there, a short distance apart, listening to the sounds of the woods and the lake. From a distant ridge a fox barked sharp and clear, pushing a rabbit along fast. An owl hooted and over by the feeder brook, that wound down from the hills, a beaver hooked his long, pointed teeth into some green wood.

"Funny how you hear things so clear at night," I said. "I remember in the army how they used to give us demonstrations—cripes, you could hear a stick snap a mile off."

The raft dipped slightly and I knew she was moving away from me, to the other side.

"You're a heel," she said quietly. "Or you wouldn't have let me come out here like this."

"I don't get it."

"Like I am, with just a—well, with what I have on."

I dropped my legs over the side of the raft and let my feet paddle around in the water. The water was a lot warmer than the air and I stopped shivering.

"It was your idea," I reminded her. "You invited me out here for dinner and then you wanted to go swimming."

"I'd been drinking," she said. "You know that."

Something cold and stiff moved up along my spine. She was sober now and she was twisting it up so that it looked all wrong. The haze was gone from her mind and she was thinking clear, real clear, about how she'd never done anything like this before and what her mother and father would think if they knew. It scared me. It scared me for sure. All she had to do was pass them the word that I'd got her lit and the next thing she knew she was out there on the raft alone with me and naked. I was pretty certain I could get away with plenty, but that was one time up that I knew I'd be called out on strikes.

I sat there thinking about her, cursing her, and wishing I'd gone to bed with Janet or got drunk or done something else. I had myself sitting right in the middle of a ripe melon patch, almost ready for picking, and now I had to go and pull a stunt like this.

How dumb can one man get?

"I didn't mean to do anything wrong," I said. "You ought to know that, Beverly."

"It seems so—awful," she said. "Sitting here like this. I—I wouldn't even do it with a bunch of girls."

She was a nice kid and she didn't know what it was all about and she had me in a spot. But I hadn't come up from Clarke Street for nothing, I hadn't gotten this far without knowing when to take a chance. She'd rolled out the barrel and she had me laying across it. I had to do something and I had to do it fast. And I knew what I was going to do.

I pulled my feet up out of the water and slid across the raft toward her. I didn't stop until I was right up close, until she was a dull blur and the smell of her wet body was all around.

"I wish you wouldn't cry," I said.

"I'm not crying, Johnny."

"Then stop thinking of things that'll make you cry. There isn't anything wrong."

"Please!"

I moved a little closer.

"Maybe I'm the wrong kind of a guy for you," I said. "Maybe I shouldn't be talking this way to you. Hell, the way I had to work, I'm lucky I finished high school. I'm not smart— not smart the way you are. I don't even know what kind of a fork to use when I get out to eat. When they say come formal I don't know whether to wear a tux or a raincoat."

I kept on talking and I kept moving in on her. I told her how much fun she was and how I liked her so much and why I hadn't told her before. I said that we were almost alike, or we wouldn't be there like this, and that we'd had a lot of fun and we hadn't ought to spoil it now.

"I like you, too," she murmured.

"You don't have to fight it, baby."

I worked in about the agency and how I liked her father and all the good things I wanted to do for him. All the time I kept getting nearer. Until I could feel the heat of her body. Until I could hear her deep breathing. Until I touched her smooth skin and the rockets went off.

"Johnny! Johnny!"

I pulled her head around and mashed my mouth down on her lips. At first she tried to push me off but I kept boring in, going after her, and pretty soon her lips parted and her tongue came out, stabbing at me.

She moaned a little as I took my mouth away and buried my face in her hair, against her neck, kissing her. I brought my left hand up and touched one of her breasts. She trembled and clung to me.

"Baby," I said. "Baby, I love you."

At a time like that, who could be sure?

She got her hands in my hair and pushed my head around so that I had to kiss her again.

"We shouldn't, Johnny."

"You're not afraid?"

"I don't know."

I kissed her again and my hand moved lower. She tried to hold my wrist, but she touched my bare skin, way down, and she took her hand away. She stiffened for an instant and then she let out a sigh and pressed her body against mine.

"You knew all the time, didn't you?"

"Not until now."

"Neither did I."

She was awkward and I hurt her and she cried a lot. My knees burned against the hard planks, and the night and her flesh closed in. She called me a bastard and said that she loved me and she bit me a couple of times. All I could think about was what this was going to cost me—some day, some time—only I couldn't stop it, I had to go on, because this was the only way for me.

She still had her arms around me when we lost our balance and fell off the raft into the lake.

CHAPTER XI

Office Party

THE PARTY got going real good around four. You start something like that right after lunch and everybody's full of food and they feel out of place and they don't drink much. But after a while somebody starts telling a joke, a clean joke, and they all listen. Five jokes later you can say anything that comes into your head.

"We oughta have these things more often," Sammy Grick told me. "Only next time let me bring my own girl. With her, I know how far I can go. If she'd been here, I'd have had her in one of those closets an hour ago."

I laughed and slapped Sammy on the back. He tried so damned hard to make you think he was important and that the women were taking their dresses off all over the place for him.

"Hey, Johnny!"

I swung around and saw Julie coming toward me. We were having the party in the back office, with all the desks and the other junk pushed up against the walls out of the way. She came across the open space, her heels high and clicking, her body hugged tight in a yellow dress. The material was so thin that I could see the dark shadows of the nipples on her breasts trying to beat their way through.

"Telephone, Johnny."

Abe Wulderstein was half drunk and he grabbed her and started dancing. She gave a mock sign of defeat and tried to go along with him. I gave her a big wink and stepped into my office and closed the door.

Janet was on the other end and she was hotter than a shotgun lying in the sun.

"You stop calling me at the restaurant," she said. "Every time I go in there they've got messages for me."

"Well, there isn't any other place to leave them."

"You know where I live, Johnny."

I did. But since that night on the raft I'd been busier than a hound dog on the track of two rabbits.

"Besides, I've got to give up work," she said. "I won't be working after Sunday."

The blood in my veins froze into a long icicle.

"What's the matter?"

"Nerves," she said. "The doctor says I'm sort of run down."

"Nothing else?"

Her laugh came along the wire, breaking up into little pieces.

"You don't have to worry about that, Johnny. The doctor thinks I couldn't get that way if I wanted to."

My blood thawed out in a hurry.

"Well, I'll get around to see you," I said. "You keep the old light lit and I'll throw stones against your window some night."

"Always breaking your neck to be funny!"

"Not me. I'll be around."

"Well, I won't be here," she said. "I'm going to get myself a little room, cheaper than where I am, and rest and think things over. That's why I called you. To say good-bye."

"Good-bye," I said.

"You're a stinker, Johnny."

"I know it."

"If I make up my mind that I really love you, you won't ever hear from me again."

"That's crazy," I said.

"But if I can make myself realize that you're just a heel—a no-good, stinking heel—I'm going to forget what I promised you and I'm going to Mr. Connors."

"Hey, now!"

"You've made my life hell, Johnny! You've slept with me and lied to me—and, I think, hated me. Nothing you've ever done, nothing you've ever said—"

"Cut it out!"

"—has ever had any truth in it. All you ever wanted from me was—"

"Shut up, you little bitch!" I shouted into the phone. "Shut up and listen to me, will you? If you try—if you think you can—"

"Good-bye, you bastard," she said and hung up.

I stood there holding the phone, cursing her out loud. I'd called her a bitch and I'd been right. All of her innocent, make-believe, I-love-you-only-you slush had been so much crap. Of course, I'd lied to her and I'd slept with her and, sometimes, I'd hated her. She'd been playing it all the way and I'd only been fooling around, afraid of what she might do, but we'd both known that. She had no right to blow a fuse just because I'd been hung up higher than a tree limb the last few nights. I'd left notes for her that I'd been busy. I hadn't lied to her. I'd been so busy that already I needed a vacation.

Before I returned to the party I called Beverly out at the lake.

"I'll be a little late," I said. "We've got a rat race going on down here."

She laughed.

"Maybe I'll run in to the movies."

"Okay."

"Want me to meet you in town for dinner?"

"I might not get out of here very early," I said. "If it's all right with you, I don't think I'll come out tonight."

"What about tomorrow?"

"Well, say, around noon. We could have a picnic some place. How does that sound?"

"Lovely!"

"Fine. Now, give me a kiss."

She gave me a kiss over the wire. I gave her one in return. We both laughed and hung up.

It was a real pain going out there to see her all the time but it was something that had to be done. She wasn't worried about that night on the raft, or what had happened on the beach and in her bedroom afterward, because she said that we were in love and that it wasn't anything to be ashamed of. But she made it real plain that she didn't want it to happen any more—not until her mother and father were home and we could get married and climb into bed legally. All of which suited me fine. If things went all right, by the time her old man got home she could sleep by herself and I wouldn't even miss her.

I grinned and went back to the party.

Somebody had borrowed a record player from the five-and-ten downstairs and there was a real hot number going on it. Skippy was out there in the middle of the floor, bumping them out. Her dress was up high and the room was shaking because she was so heavy. One of her heavy breasts had slipped its moorings and I thought it was going to spill out of the top of her blouse at any moment. She looked like all the whores in the world put together.

"Take the girdle off!" somebody shouted. "Take everything off!"

I went over and knocked the needle away from the record.

"Simmer down," I told them. "You want to throw it all away in five minutes?"

Sammy Grick put his hand in the wrong place and Skippy belted him one. Then she went over and sat in a chair and started to cry. I guessed that she was drunk.

Julie came up and took hold of my arm. Her lips were moist and freshly painted and her face was flushed.

"Why don't you break this up, Johnny?"

"Okay."

"It can't go on forever."

I looked around at the empty beer cans on the floor and the place where a bottle had been kicked over.

"Puts me in mind of the front yard back home," I said.

"I'll help you clean it up."

"You don't have to."

"I haven't got anything else to do."

I told them all to have one for the road and then to get the hell out. The girls got Skippy off into a corner and tried to straighten her out. She got sick in a wastebasket and somebody slapped her across the face. She got up and jammed her hat down over her head and left under her own power.

The guys hung around a while longer, talking about how much business they had lined up for the next week. The six o'clock whistle blew and they began thinning out. By six-thirty Julie and I were all alone.

"I don't know where to start," I said, glancing at the junk all around.

"Well, you pick up the bottles and I'll get a broom."

We worked at it steadily and it didn't take us very long. The floor needed mopping but the night man could do that. I left a note for him by the door and an envelope with five bucks in it.

"I'm pooped!" Julie said and dropped, slightly sprawling, into a chair.

"Maybe we should have a drink for the road."

"Just a small one."

I fixed a couple of balls and carried one over to her.

"I didn't know you drank whiskey, Johnny."

"Only on special occasions."

"Is this one of them?"

I put one of the glasses in her hand. She lay far back in the chair, not moving. The thin dress slid down between her legs, forming a long wide canyon. Her face was still flushed and her eyes were alive with sparkle.

"Maybe," I said.

"It is for me." She sat up quickly and tasted her drink. "I think I'll celebrate. You going to drink with me?"

"Sure."

We lifted our glasses.

"To me," she said. Her smile slipped away and her eyes clouded over. "To a Clarke Street whore!"

I knocked the glass out of her hand and she screamed. The liquor sloshed down the front of her dress, soaking in. She jumped with the cold of it and then she started to laugh.

"So you wouldn't drink to that?"

"Of course I wouldn't."

"Well, that's what Dooder called me last night."

"Who's Dooder?"

"He wanted to marry me." She choked up for a moment. "Until he found out about the baby. He changed his mind."

"The guy with the pipeline?"

She nodded.

"To hell with him."

She nodded again.

I stood there watching her, afraid of what I wanted to do, scared of how I felt about her. She was all the good and all the bad of all women in one package. I didn't try to think of any lie I could tell her so I could get what I wanted. I didn't grab her and try to find out how far I could go. I just felt so damned sorry that she'd been kicked around and I wanted her to know it and I didn't know now to tell her.

"The world's just one big Clarke Street," she said miserably.

I took out my handkerchief and bent down, trying to wipe some of the liquor off her dress. I touched her breasts, one at a time, and they were full and soft. Later, I used the handkerchief to get the sweat off my forehead.

"You'll meet some real jerks," I told her. "A good guy wouldn't let a thing like that stand in his way."

"You know what he said—after he asked me and I told him?"

"No."

She put her head down in her hands and I knew she was crying. A kid from Clarke Street didn't cry unless she'd caught it right in the teeth. "He said I ought to give him some."

"The dirty bastard!"

I got down on my knees, beside her chair, and I pulled her head over onto my shoulder. I could feel the wet of her tears through my seven-fifty shirt. I held her like that for a long time.

"You know something, Johnny?" she asked, straightening, putting a wrist up there and digging the rest of the tears out of her eyes. She bent over and kissed me lightly on the cheek. "You're not such a bad guy, after all."

"It took you a long while to say that."

"Maybe I've kept remembering too much—about how you used to be."

"That could be it."

"I guess the army did you some good."

"Yeah."

It had taught me how to polish my shoes and shine buttons—and kill. It had taught me how to take the consequences when a lie came out the wrong hole.

I fixed another drink and we talked some more about it, the warm summer nights when we used to play along Clarke Street, the pennies we used to pick up off the lot after the carnival had been to town, the gypsies who used to come through with long cars and light fingers.

"And you used to fish a lot," she said.

"Yeah."

"I remember how sick your mother got."

It all came back, how scared I'd been, and I wanted to slam her one in the mouth. I'd gone fishing, one June day afternoon, and my luck had been lousy and I'd started home without anything. Then, in a tiny cove along the river bank, I'd found a fish. A bass. A great big dead bass. I'd thought about it a long time and how drunk the old man was and that there wasn't much to eat in the house. I'd been fourteen and I'd been afraid of being hungry and I'd taken the bass home. That night we'd been sick, throwing up all over the place, and the doctor had blamed the water and the cesspool next door.

"I saw you take that fish out of the water," Julie said. "That's how I knew."

"We don't have to talk about it."

"And there were other things, Johnny—like the time you worked for that awful woman down the street. The fellows used to know and they used to tell about it, laughing, bragging about how reckless you were. It—sort of scared me. It made me think that there wasn't anything you wouldn't do."

She was almost right but I didn't think I'd bother telling her so.

"It's great to know I can forget all that," she said. "It's nice to see a person come up from the street and get to be somebody. Why, almost any college man would be crazy to have a job as good as yours!"

"You can say that again."

I started to pick up her glass but she shook her head. We were real close and she smiled at me and I knew that she meant it. Her lips were red and her teeth were white and her eyes were the color of a sun drenched sea.

"And you mean it, Johnny—to make good?"

"I mean it all right."

"I guess you know what you want."

She breathed deep and her breasts billowed up hard and pointed. She moved slightly and the dress rode down between her legs and I could see the gentle swell of her stomach. I put my hands on the back of the chair and bent over her until my mouth was only a couple of inches from her rounded nose.

"You're damned right I know what I want!" I said.

She tried to get away but I grabbed her and held her fast. It was like one of those nights along the street when I'd pulled her back between a couple of houses, reaching inside her blouse with one hand and holding the other over her mouth. Only now I was trying to make the grade with the passion of a gentleman and she was fighting me off like a lady.

"Johnny! Somebody's at the door!"

"Damn the door!"

"Please!" she whispered, holding my hand. "Let's not spoil it."

She didn't turn her head as I kissed her lightly on the lips.

"Okay," I said. "I'm sorry."

She laughed and stood up.

"It's not a bad routine," she said. "Only I get tired of it after a while."

"Maybe I'll change it some day."

"How?"

"I'll stop losing."

She picked up the glasses and put them out of sight.

"Don't count on it," she said.

I could see the shadow of someone on the other side of the frosted glass in the door. The knocking started again. I went across the room, swearing, and pulled the door open.

The first thing I noticed about this girl was the way she was dressed. She wore a gray suit that was cut tight and piled up in a heap on her chest. She was fairly tall, about five-eight, and the rest of her body seemed to be all there. The next thing I noticed about her was her face, a smooth face with that country club look—not Saturday night country club, but Sunday afternoon country club.

"Mr. Reagan, please." Her voice was a trifle sharp and very clear. "I'd like to see Mr. Reagan."

"It's late," I said. "The office is closed."

"Are you Mr. Reagan?"

"Yes."

I didn't have to get out of her way. She just slid around me and came inside.

"I'm Cynthia Noxon," she said.

"That's nice," I told her.

Julie slung her handbag over her shoulder and waved at me on her way out.

"See you Monday, Johnny."

"Yeah."

Another weekend shot to hell.

"Sorry that I broke up your fun," the girl said, shaking the curls in her dark hair so that I could see that she had some. She picked up one of the empty glasses, inspected it and smiled. "Tea and crumpets."

"Scotch on the rocks. Bourbon in the raw. Beer out of a can. Name it and you can have it."

She had a laugh that bothered me; it was like the final notes of a beautiful song, a song that leaves you sick and weak because you know, almost for certain, that there are some things you can never have.

"Perhaps later, Mr. Reagan. After we have talked business." She lit a cigarette, watching me through the smoke. "I'm sorry I was so late getting here, but traffic was very heavy out of the city."

"That's all right."

"You are interested in developing an agency for the Family Protective Insurance Company, aren't you?"

"Sure. I talked with some guy in their home office the other day and he said the boss would be up to see me."

She smiled and studied the end of her cigarette.

"That's right," she said. "Well, I'm the boss, Mr. Reagan. And I'm here to see you."

I walked across the room and stood in front of her. I found a cigarette in my shirt pocket but I didn't have any matches. I took her hand and held it up, leaning down to meet it, and I lit mine from the one she balanced between two painted fingernails. She kept watching me, a faint smile on her lips, and I knew that she wasn't going to be easy.

"Okay," I said. "Let's talk."

CHAPTER XII

Insurance Racket

IT WAS a beautiful swindle. You could give them a transfusion of hope and bleed them of their dollars—both at the same time—and they wouldn't know the difference.

We sat in a little bar off Fourth Street, picking the steak out of our teeth and putting the drinks away. We kept going over it again and again, polishing it up here and there, and every time it sounded better.

"You don't need very much money," Cynthia Noxon said. "Eight or ten thousand ought to do it."

"Hell," I said, "you could do it on nickels."

"Not with a radio program."

"Yeah, that's right. With a radio program you've got to lay out some dough."

"Just lay out the money," she said. "Don't try it with the singer."

"You don't have to talk that way. I wasn't even thinking about it."

She held her head back and laughed. The soft lights rode across her face, painting it red, and I could see the little pulse in her throat. She'd removed her suit coat and the blouse she had on was so thin she might as well have been wearing a hairnet.

"Let's get one thing straight, Mr. Reagan."

"It was to be Johnny and Cynthia."

"Okay. Johnny. Now, let's get one thing straight—about me and about Gail Dawn whom I'm suggesting for your program. I know your kind, Johnny. I've met you before and I know what you want. You're after two things. Money and women." She paused and let that sink in, then she went on, slowly. "In this league you only get money, Johnny. Count the rest of it out."

"Stop patting yourself on the back," I told her, getting sore. "Wait until you get an offer before you start putting a fence around it."

"You mean—you wouldn't?"

I leaned across the table, staring at her.

"That's right," I said. "I wouldn't."

A guy had to expect something like that from a girl who'd pulled herself up by her brassiere strap. She'd told me something, during dinner, about her old man. He'd jumped into the clip insurance business when it was young and a company could get licensed without Dewey getting all excited about it. The company had been sitting on a pile of rocks when the old man took a rope he found handy and tossed it over an extra high limb. His daughter had slunk back from college, bitter and determined, and she'd put her little round bottom right down in the middle. Lord only knew how many advertising men she slept with to get all those ads in the magazines, but she must have been pretty good at it because she blew in a sizeable fortune in the first six months. She advertised accident and sickness insurance for less than the price of dirt and pretty soon they were using wheelbarrows to take the mail to the post office. A short time after that she put on agents, guys who banged on doors and smoked out those who were too stupid to send in their money. After that came the radio program and direct mail and a dozen other gimmicks.

The waiter came over and gave us another drink. After he was gone she leaned back, stretching, letting me look at her.

"I'm glad we got that settled," she said. "I know you're going to be a knockout at this stuff, Johnny."

"That's some crystal ball you've got."

"I said before that I knew your kind. You're brutal. You don't care. You'd do anything."

I let that one go and finished my drink. The place was beginning to fill up, the early evening crowd pushing up to the bar and having a fast one before going to the movies.

"Where were we?" Cynthia Noxon asked.

"You just finished telling me your life history. And I didn't make a nickel out of it."

She laughed and it sort of frightened me, just as it had before.

"You're going to have your office here in town, Johnny?"

"No," I said. "Waymart. That's only fifteen miles away."

"But it's a smaller place."

"That's my business, I think."

She shrugged.

"It doesn't make much difference, I guess."

"No," I agreed. "It doesn't."

It made a hell of a difference. I couldn't set up an office in town, right nearby, and start hiring agents and throwing Connors' money into something that didn't belong to him. I could borrow twenty-five thousand or so from him—interest free and without his knowledge—and it wouldn't bother anybody if they didn't know about it.

"There's one thing you have to understand," she said. "We don't pay any more claims than we have to."

"You're not telling me anything new; I read one of your policies."

"It's a limited policy, you know."

I grinned.

"Limited to damn few accidents and sicknesses."

"What do they want for twenty dollars a year?"

"Sure," I said. "If they don't want to get hurt, or sick, the way the policy says, that's their business."

"We're going to get along," she said. "We won't have any trouble at all."

"Not if the commission scale is right. And the renewals."

An agent knocks himself out to make first year commissions, but that isn't the most important part of the business. It's the dough you get after the first anniversary, year in and year out and without doing any work for it, that counts.

"Forty and twenty-five," she said. "You can set up your own scale for your agents. In addition to that, there's an additional charge to the policyholder the first year—three dollars, making the whole thing twenty-three—and that you can keep or pass on to the writing agent."

"That's three bucks they'll never see," I said.

"Suit yourself."

"I will."

I dug out a mental tape and let the cash register in my head go to work. If I paid the agents twenty percent first year commission, that would leave me five bucks, plus the three, or a total of eight. If each agent could sell two a day—and a good talker ought to do five or six—I could make myself a fast dollar. Renewals were something else again but I should be able to give them ten and that would leave me fifteen.

"They'll never know what hit them," I said.

"Who?"

"The jerks up here in the sticks. They'll go for this Provider policy like I was driving them out of the hills with a scatter gun."

"There's other people in the business, too, you know."

"Not here," I said. "Not with the kind of crap you've got. Not the kind of policy that promises you the world for peanuts and then slaps you flat on your face when you start grabbing. The Met and the Pru pound on their drums once in a while, but they have good stuff and they charge for it. Besides, a lot of these miners around here—they work in the lead mines and some other place where they dig lime—can't qualify for regular protection. Then, we've got a lot of colored people around and they buy this stuff by the pound."

She nodded and gave me a big smile.

"You've studied it out."

"Sure."

"All I say is God help them, Johnny!"

We laughed about that and had another drink. I felt good. This was the road into the promised land and it was all green lights ahead. Connors was over in Europe poking around in the rubble of World War II and I had my hands in his money up to my wrists. This chick across from me had a plan of legalized robbery that would get me in the habit of running to the bank twice a day. She had the body of a goddess and the heart of a reptile and she wouldn't give a damn what I did.

"How much is this singer going to cost me?" I wanted to know.

"One-fifty a week."

"Tell her to drop dead."

"Look, Johnny," she began, leaning across the table. The top of her blouse flopped out, hanging open, and I didn't bother looking at her face. "There's something you've got to learn about this dodge—a lot you've got to learn. One of them is that you've got to advertise. Having somebody on the radio is one way of doing it—but that somebody has to be right. She is. She sings these knuckle-head songs that are liked by the kind of people you'll have to do most of your business with. Myself, I don't like 'You, You, You,' or any of that slop. But the public does, Johnny. And the public buys our policies. You've got to cater to them."

"I guess I see what you mean."

"You'd have to hire someone," she insisted. "Up here you'd only get the kind of talent that ought to be lugging a broom. This girl is tops, Johnny. She's had plenty of experience on the radio, played in a couple of movies and even did a stint in burlesque."

"What's she want to come up here in the sticks for?"

"Like a lot of girls, she took them off once too often." Cynthia lit a cigarette and leaned back, studying me. "She thought she'd like to calve up here in the hills."

"How nice."

"But that's six or seven months off. In the meantime, she can do you lots of good."

"She can't do me any good," I said.

"Stop being filthy."

We talked some more about the singer and she told me how much the girl had helped their sales when she'd been slamming her tonsils against a mike for them. I finally told her

I'd go along with it. What the hell, she only cost one-fifty a week and it wasn't my money, anyway.

The waiter returned with some more drinks. We'd been there long enough so that he knew our schedule and he didn't bother asking any more. He just made regular stops, like a train, and we took on some more cargo. The steak had been good and I didn't feel the whiskey very much, but this Noxon dame was rocking at the heels and her face was getting plenty wild.

"You staying over tonight?" I wanted to know.

She gave me a silly smile.

"If I was, you'd be the last one I'd tell, Johnny."

I thought about my old man and what he'd said and how wrong he'd been. He'd said a guy ought to just lay 'em and pay 'em. I'd found out that he was only fifty percent right. Half the time you didn't have to shell out a nickel.

"Maybe we could do the town," I said.

"Un-uh. With me, it's strictly business."

"Okay. You don't know what you're missing."

"I know what I'm missing."

The waiter made another stop, but she waved him off. We talked about the contract and when would be the best time to sign it. We decided on her office in New York because I'd have to drive down for supplies and stuff like that.

We were just getting up when I saw Julie and this guy coming from the back on their way outside. I'd never seen this Dooder she'd been talking about but I guessed it to be him. He was a big guy with a workingman look and a red face beneath sandy-colored hair. He was staggering some and she pushed him off, saying something to him, and he laughed. They went outside without seeing us.

"One for the road?" I asked, stopping at the bar.

"Okay."

We had a quick one and she said her car was down the street, past the movies.

"If you want to stay here," she said, "that's okay."

"I can always come back."

"I wouldn't go so early, only I want to drive home yet to-night." She stifled a yawn and patted her hair into place. "Frankly, I'm getting tired of working seven days a week."

"You must be crazy after money."

"Who isn't?"

We finished our drinks and wandered outside. The first show crowd was spilling out of the theatre up the street, scattering along the darkened store fronts lining the block.

"Most places the shops stay open Friday nights," she said, taking my arm.

"Not this berg. They don't know when it's Friday."

We walked slowly, stumbling over kids with popcorn, pushing around groups of chattering women who were stacked together like bunches of sour grapes.

"I thought they censored the pictures," one old bag was saying. "But did you see the way that one girl walked? Disgraceful!"

I looked at the sign over the theatre. The picture was Niagara. I gave the sidewalk critic another glance. She had the sex appeal of a totem pole set full length in concrete.

We were almost past the alley when I heard someone cry out from the shadows. I stopped real quick, bringing Cynthia Noxon up short, and stood there listening. After I heard it again I went over to the mouth of the alley.

There was a light down there, maybe fifty feet away, and I could see a couple of shadows moving around. One looked like a girl and the other like a man but I couldn't be sure at that distance. Then one of the figures fell down, the other jumped on top of it and there was a muffled scream.

"I'll see you next week in New York," Cynthia Noxon said as I pushed into the alley.

"Okay."

I found the two bodies tangled up in a bunch of old lettuce leaves in back of a fruit store. They were deep in the gloom and I couldn't see well enough to tell what was going on. The man was on top and he was swearing and breathing hard and the girl underneath was crying a little and praying a lot.

I reached down and pulled the guy to his feet.

"Hey, here, now—"

I recognized him right away and I hit him just as quick. It wasn't a real solid punch, just a left alongside his molars, but it turned him around and put him on the other side of the alley.

"For God's sake, Julie!" I said, reaching down to pick her up. "You're a big girl now."

And, then, I saw how her face was bloody and scratched and the way her dress was torn, letting one breast thrust up at me, naked and red, like it was growing out of the ground.

"Oh, Johnny, don't let him near me!" she begged. "Don't let him near me!"

I was helping her up when he came up behind me and hit me with the board. I knew it was a board because I could hear it break across the top of my head. My skull sunk in two inches and then jumped out four leaving nothing but pain and a lot of colors. He called me a four letter word and corked me one over the kidneys as I put her back down real easy, like she was going to break.

He was a big guy and he was crazy mad but he didn't know what he was up against. He didn't figure on me thinking, all in one second almost, how I'd chased her, too, trying to make a home run and how lousy and cheap it looked right then. I thought of her and the kid and the decent way she tried to live, I thought of Clarke Street and a girl named Janet and how Julie was a symbol of what Janet wanted to be. I thought of a rich guy and his daughter and how good the girl felt she was simply because she was thoughtful enough to ask a man into her bed. And I thought of a fast talker named Cynthia Noxon, but I didn't spend much time on her. I was busy thinking of something else. I was thinking about this in the alley and what the girl down there meant to me and how I'd have to do everything to make myself right for her.

I ripped around, keeping low, and the red poured down over my eyes. He swung the board again and I took it out of his hand and threw it off into the blackness. He moved backwards, bent down like a crab, trying to get his hands onto something else.

"You lousy bastard!"

In the army I had prayed to kill men and now I prayed not to kill. I could hear her crying, low and soft, and I could hear people shouting as they came running down the alley. But the only thing I could see was this guy's white face and the way he kept low to the ground, backing up.

"You can only go so far," I said. "After that you're finished."

I saw his hand go into his pocket and I saw it come out again. He put his hand down to the ground, moving it around, like he had a switch blade and he was testing it to see if it was open.

I rushed him.

The knife raced across my ribs, slicing the flesh, but I had his wrist before he could work it around and into my belly. He was strong and he held me for a second but I crotched him with my knee and he let out a groan. I took his wrist down and back and kept on going with it. He started to scream like a horse caught in a fire. He stopped screaming when his wrist snapped. He didn't try to bother me any more after that.

I pushed between the silent kids and the white faced men and women and went over to her. She stood off to one side and she'd pulled her dress together in some way. She came into my arms and held on tight.

"Don't cry, baby," I said. "Don't cry at all."

But she did and I had to wait until she was finished.

"Why are men such brutes, Johnny?"

"I don't know."

She shuddered and kissed me on the cheek.

"Thanks, Johnny."

A cop came along and pried us apart. He had a notebook and he asked me my name, a few other questions and then said we'd both have to appear in local court on Monday morning. We told him we'd be there and he started yelling at the people to clear out of the alley.

They all went except five. The cop. The misfit lying in a stupor on the ground. Julie. Me. And a fireball named Beverly Connors.

"How was the movie?" I asked her, stupidly.

Her high heels kicked up about nine dollars worth of public property.

"Busy!" she sneered. "You big clown!"

The cop told her to shut up but she didn't listen to him.

"I hope you stay busy," she said. She swung away, then turned quickly to face Julie. "Common slut!" she spat.

I watched her go up the alley. I got a cold feeling in the pit of my stomach.

"The girl's in love with you," Julie said.

I thought about that.

"Maybe."

"I know it," she said. "That's what makes a woman hate so much."

I thought about it some more. I also thought about my job and the deal I had cooking and a couple of other things. I hoped that Julie was right.

She'd damn well better be right.

CHAPTER XIII

Stop Thief

LESS THAN A WEEK later I broke ground in Waymart. I rented office space over a liquor store, threw in a truck-load of snappy new furniture and sat down to wait. Three hours after the local paper hit the streets I started signing up agents. They liked what they saw—but they didn't know what they were getting.

"You sure ask a lot of questions," one guy said.

He was right. In the first place I wouldn't touch anybody who hadn't previously been licensed to sell accident and sickness insurance with a nine foot contract. In New York State an agent has to have a slip of paper that says he knows what he's doing. He has to pass an examination to get it. And I wasn't running any educational program. I was out for blood.

I nailed six of them that first day. They ate up that fifty-dollar-a-week drawing account and the "liberal" first year commissions. I gave them their first week's pay, in advance, when they signed up and I handed them a bunch of applications to fill out on the way home. They were so damned stupid that they didn't even bother to read their contracts. They didn't know that the drawing account was only an advance and if they didn't write enough business to cover it they'd be finished at the end of four weeks. They also didn't bother to read the print where I took a chattel on everything they owned so that I could get back whatever might be due me. They were suckers. Like the jerks they were going out to sell. Like most people who want to get something for nothing.

They could go to hell.

I had supper in a fish joint down the street but the food was lousy and I didn't feel like eating anyway.

I stopped at the pay phone on the way out and called the Connors office. Julie answered.

"Hi, baby!"

I'd been giving her that baby stuff ever since that night in the alley but it hadn't done me any good.

"Hello, Johnny."

I still had a sore spot across my ribs, where the knife had dug in. I wondered if Dooder's wrist felt as good. He'd blown town right after the fracas and he hadn't shown in court. They hadn't even told me not to do it again.

"How's it going, baby?"

"Terrible!"

"You're working late."

"I can't balance, Johnny. I've been over the agent's stuff for the last couple of days and—"

She went on talking, almost crying, saying how there was something wrong and she couldn't find it. I started to sweat, cursing myself because I'd stuck her on the books. I'd told her just to put down what she saw, not worry about balancing them, and now she was doing it all backwards. She was checking.

"Look," I said. "Wrap it up for tonight. I'll get at it in the morning and fix it up."

"Well, if you say so, Johnny. I've got a woman with the baby and—"

"Great! I'll pick you up at your house in a couple of hours and we'll buzz out into the country."

She was silent for so long that I thought she'd hung up.

"How about that, Julie?"

"Thanks, no," she said. "Not tonight, Johnny."

I tossed the receiver at the phone and walked out. I cut across the street, looking up at the sign in the office window. The Family Protective Insurance Company. A fortune at the end of a sure shot chance.

I went up the stairs and kicked the door open. I went inside and stopped.

"Well," I said. "How do you like this?"

She had red hair, blue eyes and a cheap little body in a high class dress.

"Mr. Reagan?"

"Yeah."

"I'm Gail Dawn."

"Came the dawn," I said.

"That isn't very funny. I've heard it before."

"After a long, hard night, probably."

She stood up and her face looked hurt.

"I'm sorry," I said. "I talk too much sometimes."

She didn't look knocked up. She looked plenty round and soft and ready to spin. That day I'd been in New York, signing contracts with Cynthia Noxon, I'd hung around until after six waiting for this Gail Dawn to show. It'd taken her half a week to make it.

"You've got a program tomorrow," I told her. "I hope you brought your voice."

She started to give me a blast of "It's Lamp Lighting Time in the Valley," but I shut her up.

"I don't go for that kind of muck," I said.

"But that's the stuff I sing."

"I don't care what you sing. I don't want to hear it."

She put her lipstick on while she talked.

"Then don't listen to my program."

"I won't." I went over and stood beside her. "Baby, I don't care what you do as long as you sell insurance. You can do handsprings in every bed in town and I wouldn't bat an eye."

"I'll bet you wouldn't. As long as I didn't miss yours."

"Just sell insurance," I told her. "Get them writing in and you can name your own ticket."

She put the lipstick away, took out a face tissue and pressed it to her mouth.

"I'll take you up on that, Mr. Reagan."

"Okay."

I went over and sat down on the edge of a desk, watching her. She had a good selling record on the radio and I was lucky to have her show up in a hick town like Waymart. If I'd known the guy who'd fixed things up for her I'd have thanked him. He'd driven her right out into the bushes.

She'd left her luggage down at the railroad station. I drove her there, picked up the stuff, and then cruised uptown to the Hotel Dillion. A fifty-year-old bus boy came out and lugged her junk inside.

"I'll be over early in the morning," I said.

"Suit yourself." She paused on the hotel steps and looked back, smiling. "But it isn't necessary. I'll find the radio station and get to work. I think I know what you want, Mr. Reagan."

The wind caught at her dress and she didn't look so bad standing there in the half-light.

"What?" I wanted to know.

"Suckers," she said, still smiling. "By the truck-load."

I drove down Main Street to Route Seventeen, turned right and burned the tires up going south.

It was a good night and the road was wide and clear. The duals under the Ford snarled as the needle climbed around the clock.

I grinned and lit a cigarette. I was in business.

There's a lot of headaches in starting an insurance agency on somebody else's money. You have to play the angles tight to your chest and you can't let yourself become nervous. Maybe that's why I was driving so fast, so that I didn't have much time to worry about what Connors might do if he ever found out that I'd short changed his bank account twelve thousand bucks. Besides, I didn't have to worry about that. If things went okay I'd get it back to him before it was ever missed. If things went okay. If Beverly didn't start getting ideas from someplace and began writing the wrong kind of letters to her old man.

"The little bitch!"

It's funny the feeling a guy gets when he has to make time with some dame he hasn't got a real yen for. It's like strangling yourself with one hand. It feels so good when you can stop doing it.

She hadn't called me and I hadn't called her and I was getting worried about it. Although Waymart was twelve miles away there was bound to be some noise about my agency, sooner or later. I was getting set to run right through the middle of it. She'd listen a whole lot better if I could throw the sheets back and tell her about it in the dark. And, of course, I could do worse. I could sleep alone.

I hadn't heard from Janet since the night we'd talked on the phone. I was crying about it. For joy.

When I got back to town I stopped around at the Connors office. There was still a light up there and I guessed that the old guy was up there scrubbing the floors. He wouldn't bother me any and it wouldn't take me long to jockey the books around so that they were running straight. I reminded myself to give Julie a job sitting out front, looking pretty. I'd have to work out sufficient time so that I could do the final pencil work myself. There were enough booby traps around without building another one.

I stepped out of the elevator and went through the darkened front office; the light that was burning was the one in on my desk. I wondered who'd left it on.

She didn't hear me come in. She had her head down on the desk, resting in the middle of a mess of papers, and she was crying like a kid.

"Hey, now, baby!" I stuck my hand under her chin and pulled her head up. "Cut it out, will you?"

Julie's lips quivered and her eyes filled up with more tears. I could see dark, wet spots down the front of her blue blouse. She turned away, jerking herself loose, sobbing bitterly.

I walked around the office, smoking, waiting for her to calm down. I knew what had happened. I'd been a damned fool. My feet froze fast to the bottom of my shoes.

"Johnny?"

"Yeah?"

She was standing up now, but I didn't look at her. She'd stopped crying, almost, and her voice was steady.

"You're a thief, Johnny."

"Take it easy, kid."

"You know what I found?"

"Never mind." I looked out of the window, down at the lights. "I told you to knock it off, didn't I? You sit here and beat your brains out, trying to figure something you don't understand, and then you flip your buttons."

"Listen, Johnny, I took bookkeeping in school."

"Yeah?" I said. "I had six months of Latin but I couldn't read what's on King Tut's tomb."

Her high heels snapped on the linoleum as she came over by me.

"Johnny Reagan," she repeated, "you're a common thief!"

I stopped looking at the empty street. I swung around, catching her by the shoulders. My fingers dug down into her flesh, hurting her, making her cry out.

"I told you to take it easy!"

"Please, Johnny!"

"That wasn't a nice thing for you to say."

She tried to twist loose.

"You're hurting me, Johnny. Let me go."

I let her go.

"I don't want to fight with you, Johnny."

She went over to the desk and pushed the papers together in a pile.

"You won't need them," she said. "You know what's there, anyway."

We stood there, looking at each other, the silence riding around the room on all four walls.

"I'm quitting, Johnny."

"You don't have to."

Her smile was bitter and broken. I wanted to go over there and tell her that I'd make it right and that I'd change it all in the morning. But I couldn't do that. There was that office in Waymart, the money that was already spent, and the road was wide ahead.

"I wish I'd gone when you told me to," she said. She shook her blonde head and bit her upper lip. "I wish I had, Johnny."

"Yeah."

"And I stayed for you. Just for you."

"Thanks, anyway."

"You don't have to get mad." She picked her little gray jacket up from the back of a chair. "I'm such a fool, really. I wanted to do it right—everything right—just for you. Ever since the other night I've lain awake thinking about what a great guy you are, Johnny!"

"Cut it!"

"I've been there in bed, with my window open, listening to the sounds of the street. Hearing them fight, hearing them swear, hearing their feet running fast into the shadows. And I felt good. I felt good because I thought of you, and how you'd come up from the street, shaking it off. How wrong can you be?"

"You don't have to tear yourself apart. What the hell—"

"But I want to. I want to leave it all right here."

"Suit yourself."

She put on the jacket. She buttoned it and it pulled in tight over her breasts. Her tummy was flat and her legs were long and straight and I didn't want to look at her any more.

"I kept telling myself that you've got this good job and that things have to be right. I didn't even go out for supper. I just worked, trying to find it—and I did. For God's sake, Johnny, what are you thinking of?"

"Shut up!"

"Holding back the advance payments, not putting them in the bank." Her voice rose, steadier now, whipping across the room. "Holding ordinary premiums and running them out to the end of the grace period. No wonder you fired Mr. Collins!"

I lit a cigarette. The smoke shot down my throat and boiled around inside my chest.

"Drop it!" I said. "Forget it. Tomorrow you start out front, gassing with the people that come in. Don't worry about the money. I'll do that."

I saw her coming, slow and straight and moving all over. I saw the hardness in her eyes and the way her lips twisted. I saw her hand, too, but I didn't even bother getting out of the way. It cracked alongside my face and I hardly felt it.

"You changed me the other night," she said. "You showed me in the alley how it felt to be someone and how it could be for us. I kept thinking about you, after, and hoping—and wanting you. I'd have kissed you. I'd have gone to bed for you. I'd have had a kid for you!"

A wild sensation shot up my spine, roared across the top of my head and then sat down, pounding, between my eyes. I tried to get my hands on her but she was moving away.

"But it's all over," she said huskily. "I won't steal for you. And I won't hurt you. I won't even remember you. Oh damn you, Johnny Reagan, I never want to see you again! You and your cheap lies and your rotten tricks! You and your—"

I hit her hard, clean across the face. She went backwards, bumping into the desk, her eyes deadened with fear and pain. She screamed once and ran out to the elevator, still whimpering.

I sat down, feeling sick. I thought about what lousy luck I was having at a time like this. I'd chased her like a pup in spring, ever since I'd been smart enough to follow the trail. And when I'd had her sitting out on the end of a limb I hadn't even known enough to bark at the tree.

Well, a guy has to lose once in a while.

I found a bottle of Old Grand-Dad in the desk and belted that around for a while. I had an idea that Julie wouldn't give me any trouble, like going to Connors or starting a chain-reaction story around town. She wouldn't talk about anybody else. She'd had enough of that herself.

I was part-way through the bottle when the phone started jumping around on the desk. At first I wasn't going to answer it because nobody in his right mind calls an insurance agency after five but it kept chattering away at the ragged edges of my nerves and I finally gave in.

"St. Vincent Hospital," some cutie said.

"I'm not that sick," I said. "I'm just drinking. Stick around and I'll call you later."

She thought I was real wise so she shifted her voice up into high.

"Mr. Reagan, please."

"He's not here. But I can take a message for him."

It's easier when you do it that way.

"I'm calling on behalf of Miss Janet Hobbs."

That really tore the night wide open. I was ready to rip the phone out and ask for a refund.

"Okay, sister. I take shorthand."

"Well, gee, aren't you clever?"

"I could show you."

She let that one ride past the end of the wire.

"Miss Hobbs is a patient in the hospital and she wanted us to get in touch with Mr. Reagan. She'd appreciate it if he would visit her as soon as possible."

"What's wrong with Miss Hobbs?"

"I'm sorry but I'm not at liberty to tell you. If you'd be kind enough to have Mr. Reagan stop around tomorrow, why—"

I hung up and tipped the bottle again. What had happened to Janet? I had another drink. Maybe she'd bent an axle, or something. I had another short one and forgot about it.

At ten o'clock I finished up the bottle and decided to stop playing around with fate. I called Beverly.

"I don't know whether I want to talk to you or not," she said.

I was drunk enough to be independent.

"Well, hang up," I told her.

"Same old Johnny!"

"That's more like it."

We used up a half a minute saying nothing.

"Sore?" I wanted to know.

The way she laughed I knew she wasn't.

"Just sorry," she said. "Sorry I scolded you."

"How sorry?"

"I've been waiting for you to call, Johnny. I feel like such an awful—fool."

"Okay."

The bottle was empty and the night was young and she was out there by herself.

"Pull the lock off the door," I said. "I'll be right out."

"You're very blunt."

"It's been a long time."

"I'll wait," she said softly. "I'll wait for you, Johnny."

I kept her waiting about an hour. I stopped at the diner on the way out of town and had ham and eggs. After four cups of coffee I began to think straight again.

I drove carefully, keeping the Ford under fifty, thinking about things. Apparently I was all square with Beverly and I shouldn't have any trouble from that quarter. But if I knew what was going on at the hospital with Janet I'd feel a hell of a lot better. Maybe she was just sick and wanted to see me—and maybe she'd be like a boomerang sailing back from nowhere. That, I decided, was the trouble with a dame like Janet. You couldn't tell which way the sparks might fly—or who might get burned.

I kept driving, feeling tired and disgusted about what had happened with Julie in the office. Then I told myself that it was over, that it was finished, that I couldn't do a thing about it. After a while I had myself sold on the idea that that's the way it would always stand.

I parked alongside the cottage and went up the steps to the porch. The front door was unlocked so I went in and closed it after me.

She lay sprawled on the davenport, reading a book. She had on a thin negligee and it slid down as she put the book aside.

"Hi," she said.

She moved her legs around, making room for me. The negligee slipped some more as she reached up and turned off the light.

"You know where to find me," she said.

I took off my clothes and left them in a heap on the floor. My eyes were heavy and I wanted to lay down almost any place and go to sleep. I went over and grabbed squatter's rights on my half of the davenport.

"Kiss me, Johnny."

I kissed her.

"Once again, darling,"

I did it some more.

"You act tired."

"I am."

I might as well have saved my breath. She wouldn't let me sleep all night long.

Sometimes life can be rugged.

CHAPTER XIV

Selling Talk

I FOUND JANET lying in a narrow white bed playing solitaire.

"Cripes," I said. "I thought you had the seven year crud, or something."

She smiled and stuck the cards under her pillow. She looked real dark, lying there against all that white—her hair, her eyes, the nut brown of her skin.

"What happened, baby?"

She glanced down at the foot of the bed, studying the way her toes stuck up in the air and made twin tents.

"I had a miscarriage," she said demurely.

I almost went out of the window on my back. Then I stopped worrying because it was all over and I guess that was the way it happened sometimes.

"I didn't know I was that way. The doctor said I—couldn't."

She'd been wrong so many times I didn't know what to think. If she was trying to cut my mortality table down five or ten years she'd made a first class start. I decided to give up on this one. She was past history.

"Well, that's too bad," I told her.

Her stare was steady and wise.

"I wish you wouldn't talk just to hear what you can say."

"All right." I sat down on the edge of the bed. "What's up? What do you want with me?"

The old hurt clouded her eyes.

"I thought you might pay the hospital bill."

"Okay."

"I don't have any hospitalization and I don't have any money."

I lit a cigarette and she told me to put it out. I kept smoking, anyway.

"You ought to have a Family Protective policy."

"You needn't sneer."

I took her gently by the shoulders and brought her around. I bent over and kissed her on the cheek. She didn't try to get away and she didn't move in any closer.

"Listen," I said, "you twist up everything I say. I'm talking about a new insurance agency I started over in Waymart. That's the name of it. The Family Protective. It's going to turn into a gold mine."

I got up and walked around the room, talking fast, and she kept watching me. I'd been tired before but now I was wide awake and I wondered why I hadn't thought of this plan right at the start. I ought to have somebody over in Waymart, watching things in my new office, and Janet didn't have any place else to go. She could answer the phone and days when I didn't get over there she could bank the money. Later on she might need some help and I could get a couple of jerky kids to work for her.

"It doesn't sound so bad," she said when I'd finished. "Only there's one thing about it, Johnny."

"Shoot!"

"No more of the—other."

Was she kidding?

"Whatever you say, baby." I went over and sat down beside her again. I held her face between my hands and looked right down into her eyes. She blinked back the wetness and gave me back a smile. "Look, Janet, we've been a couple of kids and we both know it. I've been sort of—lousy. I won't be that way any more. All I want is for you to be happy and have a job and have a chance to live like a person."

That was a big speech for me and I said it low and intimate, just as though I meant it. I wanted to get in a corner and heave. The way she kept smiling at me, her lips pink and her teeth white and her eyes bright, made me think of somebody else for just a second. Somebody I didn't want to remember.

"I won't be out of the hospital for a couple of days."

"Stop worrying about it. Whenever you get ready."

"And the bill—you'll help me with that, Johnny?"

"I'll take care of it on the way out."

"Thanks, Johnny." She put her head down on the pillow and I knew she was going to bawl. "Thanks a lot."

When I got downstairs I stopped in the office and told them to ante up the fine. The old bag in there tried to nick me for an extra ten but I pulled some addition on her and left her flat.

It was still early in the morning but I stopped in at the nearest bar and had one for luck. Putting Janet in the office at Waymart should prove to be a smart thing. There wouldn't be much come through there, except new applications, money and claims. The applications would go straight to the New York office to be written up. The money was to be forwarded once a month, after I'd taken my cut. And nobody worried about the claims. What could Janet do that could be wrong?

I had another drink and decided that I ought to drive over to Waymart and see what was going on. That thrush was supposed to have her first program that afternoon and some of the guys might show up with a few applications. I went to the phone and called the Connors office. I was told that a Miss Cynthia Noxon was waiting to see me.

I drove over there in a hurry.

I tried to get the elevator but it was on its way down and I had to wait. It finally stopped, the doors opened and Cynthia stepped out.

"Well!" she said. "The mid-morning executive!"

"Skip it," I told her. I got her by the arm and pushed her out into the street. "Don't come looking for me here again."

She pouted prettily.

"You didn't tell me not to."

"Well, consider yourself told."

It was one of those good fall days, with the early morning fog gone and the sun sinking in. She took off her coat and hung it across one arm.

"I tried to call you in Waymart, but no one answered the phone."

"That's a hot one," I said. "No one was there."

"It's a hell of a way to run an office."

"But cheap."

She had her car parked at the curb, a big red Caddy with the top down. She got in and told me to get in. It was a pleasure.

"Gail get there all right?"

"Yeah."

"You said her first program was today."

"At three-fifteen."

Cynthia Noxon sighed and started the Caddy. She gave it the gas and we barreled off down the street. I wondered where we were going and decided to find out.

"Waymart. I want to see what you've got over there."

"Okay."

She flipped the radio on.

"I'll bet you're wrong about the program time. I'll bet it's either right now or late tonight."

"All right, so I don't know what time of the day I bought," I grumbled.

She looked at me and smiled graciously. "Forgive me, Johnny, but I don't think you know anything at all about radio times—or, especially, Gail Dawn. If there's a sustaining program that can be moved, she'll move it—even if she has to get herself raped by the program director."

"I could think of a worse fate for him."

"You're not funny."

"Hell, I wasn't kidding."

We drove on a ways in silence. The air was clean and warm and the countryside sparkled in the sun.

"I'm serious about that," Cynthia said. "This Gail Dawn is a real pro. She knows that her best time is around noon or at night. It's family people she has to sell and that's when they're home. You won't find her burning up your money in the middle of the afternoon. Not that she cares about you, or me—or anybody else, really. It's a matter of pride with her. She wants to be the best damned salesman on the air. And someday she will be."

"If she doesn't stop sleeping around," I said, "she won't have time for it."

The radio came on and Cynthia began punching at the stations. She didn't get anything but news and halitosis and some dame chasing the father of her kid. The road was winding now, boring up into the mountains, and I took over as radio operator. She drove fast and the wind came in and hoisted her skirt up over her knees. She had a couple of good knees and what she had above them wasn't so bad, either. I took quite a while to find the station.

That's her!" Cynthia shouted excitedly. "Listen to that!"

To me it sounded like somebody was throwing pots and pans around a room and somebody else was yelling. But I never had gone much for that ride-the-range, light-a-candle-in-the-window stuff and I wasn't going to do any back flips just because this Gail Dawn was wearing the lining off her lungs doing it.

"Shut it off," I told her. "You want me to have a stroke?"

"They'll buy insurance from you now."

"Maybe if they thought she'd stop that screeching they would."

She started to turn the radio off, but I stopped her. I was paying that dame a hundred and fifty a week to make a public nuisance of herself. If nobody else would listen to her I might as well work overtime at it and try to get my money's worth. Pretty soon she stopped singing and I began to feel better.

She gave them the commercial herself and it was a dilly at misrepresentation. No one, unless they were familiar with Family Protective's contract, could have spotted the phony lines. She told them, in a soft and low personal way, that the policy covered everything—all kinds of sicknesses and accidents. She told them it only cost twenty-three bucks the first year and twenty after that. She was telling them the truth. That's what it cost and everything was covered—with exclusions and fine print.

"They'll indict me for robbery," I told Cynthia Noxon. "I'll wind up in jail."

"And that's probably where you belong."

We both laughed. It was great to be going at last, to have the fat in the pan, to watch the flame of success burn higher.

We went straight to the office in Waymart. Even before I unlocked the door I knew that the two phones inside were hopping around like frogs in a rainstorm.

"Listen to that money rattle!" she said, grabbing up the nearest one. "Let's get to work, Johnny!"

And it was work. All afternoon those phones kept barking. Dozens of leads. Good leads. People wanting to snap into line so they could have first crack at this great big insurance bargain. People waving their pocketbooks around so you had to trip over them. Fools. People. Jerks. The colossal jackpot.

"What an afternoon!" Cynthia said, checking the name list.

It began to slack off after five. We started putting the names and addresses on cards to be distributed amongst the agents the next morning. Around five-thirty the agents started calling in. Up until now they'd been cold canvassing—knocking on doors and yammering in the dark—and their haul had been modest. But the program had changed that. They were getting better receptions, more money, and they were hotter than shotguns after a turkey shoot.

"This is a real fertile field around here," Cynthia said, leaning back in her chair. "Real fertile, Johnny."

She leaned back nicely. She had a suggestive shape, full and soft looking, and she didn't seem to mind how many times she was undressed by my eyes.

"Well, there's a lot of coal miners around here," I said.

"And they can't get insurance of this kind anyplace else?"

"Yeah. There's farmers, too. And ordinary guys working up in the woods. All kinds."

It got dark but we didn't bother turning the lights on. We sat there talking about it and smoking. She told me how I should list the applications when I sent them down to her. She knew her business all right and she gave me a couple of angles I hadn't thought about before. It was easy to see how she had gotten so far. She hated people who were dumb—and she thought everybody was built that way.

"You ought to get some people here in the office," she said. "To help you out. There's going to be plenty for you to do."

"I've got that taken care of."

"Your job's to keep after the salesmen, Johnny. You can't let up on them for a minute. And you've got to watch them all the time. I've got a guy who used to take my leads and use them to sell silverware."

"Pretty smart."

Her cigarette bobbed around in the dark.

"Until I had him arrested." She got up and the cigarette went with her. "I don't fool around, Johnny." She kept walking around, like she didn't know what to do. "Remember that, Johnny. Always remember that."

"Sure."

We locked up the office and went out for supper. She seemed to prefer drinking to eating and that was all right with me. We put them away, one after the other, and pawed the food around a little bit. She had a wild glow in her face and eyes by the time we went out to the street and got into the car. She told me to drive and I didn't argue with her.

The Caddy had plenty of get up and go to it but I took my time. The top was still down and the night air slid down from the hills, feeling cool. She moved across the seat, a little at a time, until finally she was right up close where it was warm and I could get my hand on her.

"You keep out in center field," she said, laughing and patting my hand. "Don't try any home run stuff the first time up."

"Okay."

"You know what I mean?"

"Hell, no. Show me."

We were almost into town when I decided to get that car off the road. We'd been riding along, talking about business, and she'd crept up on me all of a sudden. Maybe it was the drinks, or the warmth of her, or something like that.

I parked at the mouth of a wood road, under some pines.

"I don't think I like this," she said.

I tried to kiss her but she wouldn't let me. She fastened her teeth alongside my cheek and I thought I'd been shot. I watched her move through the shadows to the other side of the seat and I could hear how heavily she was breathing.

"There's something you should understand," she told me, her voice sharp and tight. "I'm not everybody's whore, Johnny."

The way she said it, it made it seem wrong and dirty and awful that I'd ever stopped the car. I rubbed my cheek and lit a cigarette.

"You're a nice guy, Johnny. I like you. You've got guts and you're a hard worker and, I suppose, you'd make a fine stud."

"Yeah?"

"It's nothing to be ashamed about, Johnny." She laughed and I could tell that she wasn't mad any more. "You like your women and they like you. Only don't count me on your fingers. It's strictly business with us, Johnny. You haven't got anything I want. Remember that. And you won't ever get anything from me. Remember that, too."

The night was all around us, deep and dark. The smell of the pines filled the air and it was so quiet you could hear the field mice mooching around in the leaves. A car came along, ripping up the road. It went on past, its radio playing loud and clear. "Okay," I said.

I started the Caddy and backed it onto the highway. We drove in silence until we reached the city limits.

"Mad, Johnny?"

"Hell, no!"

"Sometimes I talk too bluntly."

We went under a street light and I glanced at her. She sat there smiling at me, real sure of herself. I supposed that she was thinking about how much money she had and how smart she was and all the other stuff that might go with it. I got the feeling that she thought I was just a little guy in knee pants.

I parked the car in front of the office. I got out and she slid under the wheel.

"Keep in touch with me, Johnny. Let me know how things go."

"Sure."

She reached up and patted my face.

"Luck, Johnny."

"Thanks."

She shot the Caddy down the street, pouring on the power. I watched the big red tail lights until they drifted out of sight. Then I went in the bar down the street and had a drink.

I couldn't put my finger on the reason, but that dame had me plenty worried.

CHAPTER XV

Rift in the Loot

FOR THE NEXT couple of months I was busier than a man shoveling water uphill. I drove the road between the Connors office and Waymart so much that I could have gone in my sleep without getting off the macadam once. It was a real race, with the rats running all over the place.

"You should get more rest," Janet told me plenty of times. "You're doing good. Why don't you take it easy?"

"Yeah."

There was plenty of money rolling into the Provider, but it had been necessary for me to buy fancy office machines and put on more help. The agents, of course, paid their own way but the chic dolls I had cluttering up the chairs and desks kept gnawing away at the hinges on the gravy train.

"Don't worry about it," Cynthia Noxon told me during one of her visits. "Just wait until those quarterly premiums start pouring in."

"I wish we could sell them all annually. When it's split up in four parts it doesn't look like anything."

"You've got to do what they want, Johnny. You have to sell it the way they'll pay."

She was right and I was right—and I wasn't making a dime. I was a little sore at her for having changed the mode of premium payments on the policy, after we started plugging it, but there wasn't much I could do about it. The way it was set up there wasn't any saving if a guy paid once a year, or four times a year, so he felt his way along as cheaply as possible. Of course, in a labor area it made the insurance easier to sell but it also made you wait for the rest of your money and you were a lot less certain about getting it.

I hoped that Connors would stay in Europe until after the resurrection.

"They're having fun," Beverly kept telling me. "Big fun! They lost five thousand dollars in one week on the Riviera."

The old bastard!

"They're going to Spain and to France and—oh, just all over!"

Well, happy days!

The weather was getting colder now and Beverly had moved back into the house at the edge of town. Sometimes we went out to dinner, sometimes we went to the movies, or dancing, and sometimes we just went to bed. Once in a while I stayed in my own apartment, drinking. When I drank I thought of Julie and when I thought of her I got so stinking sick of the whole thing that I almost wanted to chuck it. Only I couldn't. I'd gone into Connors for another five thousand, making a total of about seventeen, and I had to sit it out. Every day I found myself a quiet corner and figured out how much longer it would take. The same answer kept boring through to sit there on the paper. Six months. Until the new quarterly renewals rolled in. Six months of risk and, then—clover!

In the short space of two months I'd tripled the agency force. I had guys crawling up out of barrels and swinging from the trees. The radio program came at the suckers twice a day now and Gail kept pouring the coal to a steadily blazing fire.

"I'm worth two-fifty a week," she told me one night.

She'd stopped around to the office early, on her way to work. She'd been wearing a bright red wool suit that didn't quite conceal her secret of approaching motherhood.

"That doesn't say you're going to get it," I told her.

I'd offered her a drink and she'd shook her head.

"Go to hell, Johnny Reagan!"

In the end, I'd chased her down to the street and it'd cost me two seventy-five. She was worth it all right. She kept those phones humming and the money jumping. I didn't know what the hell I'd do when she got so big she couldn't get next to a microphone.

"You'll be out of the woods by that time," Janet told me. "You can get somebody else."

"You find them."

"I will."

Janet was a good kid and she was working like hell. I left her alone, not trying to bother her physically, and it seemed to be a sensible arrangement. She had an apartment some place on the North Side and she kept herself dressed up like a million bucks. Most of the squawks from customers were men who came into the office—usually those who'd been turned down on some claim they'd had—and she just gave them her smile and a shake of her can and things were fine. I'd raised her salary up to a hundred a week and she earned every cent of it. Without her I'd have run myself so ragged, chasing between the two offices, that I'd have been a skeleton without half my bones.

"It's starting to snow," she said one day, shortly after lunch.

I watched the white flakes peck away at the window, then turn to water.

"Yeah."

"Weather forecast says a heavy snow tonight."

"That's good. Most everybody'll be home and the fellows won't have any trouble getting interviews."

"Don't you ever think of anything except business?"

Sure, I thought, I think about Connors and his damned money and all the things that could happen if the wheel didn't stop spinning pretty soon.

"No," I said.

She was at her desk, working on the bank deposit of the day before, but she stopped doing that for a while and just stared at me.

"Why don't you take the afternoon off, Johnny? Go out and see a movie. Go out and get drunk. Go out and get—"

"Sure," I said, grinning. "It'd be fun, wouldn't it?"

She got real busy with the deposit.

"Sometimes you say the jerkiest things."

I lit a cigarette and went over to the window. The snow was coming down harder, clinging to the ledge on the building, painting the cars white in the street below.

"Maybe I will," I said.

I thought of getting back to Middlesville early, wandering around Connors' office, listening to all the smart remarks about where had I been and all the phony advice about what I should do. It came from the girls and it came from the agents and I didn't listen to any of them. I knew that lapses were up, production down. Business stunk over there—they didn't have to tell me that. But they did. They told me how it used to be and how it was now and they were sore about it. They didn't know what they were talking about. They didn't know I owned the Family Protective Agency or that I'd grown bigger in two months than most of them would grow in a lifetime. But they'd find out—some day. And when they did all hell would break loose.

"I'll leave a number for you to call," I told Janet. "In case you want me."

"All right. Have a good time."

I didn't have to look up the number or anything like that. I just wrote it down on a piece of paper and left it there. I'd been going to call her a lot of times, drunk and sober, but I'd never finished the job. I'd dialed the number and listened to the phone ring and then I'd hung up. Somehow, talking to Julie on the phone hadn't seemed to be quite right.

It was still snowing hard but the roads were good and I took it easy.

A half hour later I parked the car in front of the restaurant. I left the motor running. I sat there for a long time before I got out.

It was one of those days, white like Christmas, with things quiet and easy all around you. You get to thinking back, thinking back a long ways, and you get a little scared and angry because it hasn't been better.

There was the street—Clarke Street—cold, miserable, desolate. It was a street sitting at the edge of the world and the rim of hell. You grew up, hating it, promising all the time to make it better some day. And you missed. You missed because you stayed yourself. You became part of the street and it became part of you. You only saw the difference when you noticed the changes around you, like Julie—like a star in a clouded sky suddenly lighting up. You stood in the glow, watching the beauty, and for a while you were afraid. Then you weren't afraid any more and you began reaching for it, chasing it through the shadows of the alleys, driving yourself crazy with the want of it. When you were out of breath you started to walk, not running at all, and the light got closer, almost near enough to touch. Pretty soon you thought the light was on you, too, and you felt better and you tried to reach all the way. For just a second you stood there, washed naked by the brightness of it. Then the clouds came up again, rolling fast and dark, and suddenly the light was gone. The light was gone and you went back to doing what you had done before. Watching. Hoping. And dying just a little inside while you waited.

I got out of the car, cursing, and went into the restaurant.

She was in back of the counter, wiping off the coffee urn, and she didn't turn around when I came in. The only other person in the place was a skinny guy in white slacks who sat at a far table reading a newspaper. I walked over to the counter and sat down.

"Coffee," I said.

She put the cloth aside and picked up a cup.

"Hello, Johnny."

"A little on the light side, huh?"

"I know."

She swung around, puffing a strand of hair away from her face, and put the coffee in front of me. She had on a black uniform that fit pretty good; it made her hair look real blonde, almost the color of dead grass.

"How have you been, Johnny?"

There was nothing in her face or eyes, nothing at all to tell how she felt. She just stood there with her hands on the counter, her fingers moving slowly up and down, staring past me.

"Okay. And you, Julie?"

"Fine." Her lips twisted and she folded her hands together, fingers tight. Her breasts rose sharply and I could see the wet gathering in the corners of her eyes. "You had no business coming here," she said. "You ought to leave me alone, Johnny."

"I came to eat crow," I said.

She went back to polishing the urn.

"I don't care what you came for."

But I knew she did. The way she said it, low and soft and not full of anger, told me how it was with her. She wanted me there just as much as I wanted to be there. Only she wanted the pieces to fit, to be right.

"I came to apologize," I said. "And to ask you something else."

"I'm listening," she said.

I told her how it had been for me—or, at least, I told her almost all of it. I told her about Family Protective and how good it was going, only I said that it wasn't my kind of a business and I was getting out. All the time I was talking I kept wondering how I could sell the agency and get enough out of it to make things square with Connors. Of course, I didn't tell Julie about Beverly but that wasn't necessary. What she didn't know couldn't cause me any trouble.

"I'm not sure," she said after I finished talking.

"Not sure about what?"

"That you have half an idea what you're saying."

She made me so crazy mad I wanted to hit her over the head with a stool.

"You want me to go back outside and come crawling in through the door on my hands and knees?"

She turned around slowly and smiled at me.

"You've just done that," she said.

That made me mad some more. I asked myself how I could figure a dame like Julie. Here I was wearing my conscience on my sleeve and she couldn't see it for wise cracks. I got up and pushed the cup toward her.

"Shove it," I said.

I walked toward the door.

"Johnny!"

"Yeah?"

"Come back here, Johnny. Please come back!"

So I went back and sat down again. The guy at the table in the rear was sound asleep and he didn't hear her crying or the things I said. There were just the two of us and I kissed her when I got the chance. She didn't mind a bit. She came at me across the counter and kissed me without even asking.

"Maybe we can get someplace," I said, running my hands through her hair. "Only you have to stop being so damned sassy. We have to figure this thing out."

"I guess we know what we want," she said.

The guy in the rear continued to sleep and we talked some more. We didn't say anything about marriage, not in so many words, but we both knew it was right there, staring at us. She worried about her kid and how I felt about that.

"Look," I told her. "Don't worry about anything, Julie. We start out fresh. Anything that's happened before to either of us is cancelled out. We just accept each other for what we are now, not condemn each other for what we might have done before."

"Gee, Johnny, you're sweet!"

I kissed her again.

"Just one thing, Johnny."

"Sure."

"This is for keeps?"

"You can say that over and over!"

"Johnny!"

This time she did the kissing. Some guy out on the street looked in and saw us and knocked on the window. We laughed and waved back at him.

"There's something else, Johnny."

"Okay."

"You have to be all straightened up—before. With Mr. Connors. With yourself. We can't go into this all mixed up."

"No."

She had something there. I couldn't excuse myself from Beverly's bed and cause a rumpus while I was on her old man's hook. And I couldn't get squared off with him until I did something with Family Protective. I started to sweat. I had so much work to do I was tired already.

"It may take a little while," I admitted.

She shrugged those beautiful shoulders and went back to polishing the urn. Every time she moved her arms she shook all the way down across her hips. And every time she shook I shook with her.

"That won't stop us from seeing each other," I said.

She cocked her head and gave me a sly smile.

"Well give it a try," she promised.

I ordered another coffee and she fixed it for me. A couple of railroaders came in and yelled for eggs and bacon. The little guy at the back table shuffled toward the kitchen. The pay phone in the corner started ringing and Julie went to answer it.

"For you," she said.

I crossed to the booth and wedged myself inside.

"Hello."

"Oh, Johnny!" It was Beverly. She was crying so hard the phone almost dripped tears. "Oh, Johnny!"

"What's up?" I shouted.

"I—I just got a cable from mother. Oh—Johnny!" The temperature inside the booth shot up fifty degrees.

"They aren't on their way—home?"

"Oh, no. Nothing like that. Dad—Johnny, Dad's sick and he may die. He's in a hospital in Rome." She let out a low moan. "Johnny! Johnny!"

My nerves backfired, kicking cold, bumpy sweat out all over my body. What a miserable thing to happen! If the old guy died now there'd be an immediate accounting of the estate. It wouldn't take six months. It wouldn't take three. And I needed three—at least. I was like a guy stuck in the middle of nowhere. I had to jump one way or another.

"Johnny, didn't you hear me?"

"Yeah, yeah." Was she kidding? "I'll be right over. Just sit tight."

"Thanks."

"You're welcome, baby."

I hung up and pushed out of the booth. I looked at Julie. I glanced away, not meeting the question in her eyes. I had to take care of first things first. There was no compromise with disaster.

"Call me, Johnny." She knew I was getting out of there. "Or stop in again some time."

"Sure."

"I hope it isn't anything—serious."

"No. It isn't anything at all."

I went to the door and jerked it open. The snow came up around my ankles, falling down inside my shoes. I didn't bother looking back.

The rear tires snarled in the snow as I pushed the Ford down the street. It was a treacherous night, a night for accidents, but I drove plenty fast. It kept me busy, just staying on the road, and I didn't have a chance to think about what I'd left in the restaurant.

Which was just as well.

I'd made up my mind about something else.

I was going to marry Beverly Connors.

CHAPTER XVI

Wedding Night

THE NEXT DAY we drove down to Elkton, Maryland, and signed a lease on each other's life.

It was easy.

The Justice of the Peace was a short, fat man with a glass eye that didn't fit properly. He led us into his living room and then he called his wife from the kitchen. She came in and he told her to go out and pick up another witness. Pretty soon the wife came back with a woman who had a rag tied over her head and a dust mop in one hand.

We got through the ceremony in nothing flat. I hadn't thought I'd be nervous, but I was. I had on a new belt and every time I took a breath I could hear the leather squeak. Beverly's face was serious, almost reverent, as she stared straight at the Justice, listening to him spring the deadfall.

I put a ring on her finger and she put one on mine. I was glad mine was a size too large because I'd be able to take it off anytime I felt like it. Then I kissed her, handed the Justice twenty bucks and we were married.

"Tell your friends where I live," the old guy said as we went out.

"Sure."

After we got into the car I turned to her.

"Hello, Mrs. Reagan," I said.

She leaned toward me and kissed my mouth.

"Hello, Mr. Reagan," she breathed.

"Not sorry?"

She shook her head but her face saddened.

"Now, if dad only gets all right, why—"

I patted her hand and started the car. The night before we'd called the hospital in Rome and she'd talked to her mother. Her father had been resting comfortably, better than expected, and her mother said if he made the grade okay they'd cut short their vacation and come home.

"He'll be all right," I assured her.

She snuggled in close, putting her head on my shoulder, and I eased the Ford out into the late afternoon traffic.

"I have you," she said simply.

We drove a couple of hours before we stopped for an early dinner.

"I'm not hungry," she said. "I'm excited."

"About what?"

"You know what."

I grinned and speared a fried shrimp. She pushed her coffee aside and dabbed at her lips with the paper napkin. Her eyes were all fire.

"We could stop some place overnight," she said. "Maybe a tourist cabin. We won't be able to have a—honeymoon until you can get away for a while."

"I've got to get back."

"The place will run itself for another day."

Her old man's office had been doing that for a long time.

"I'm talking about the deal in Waymart," I said. "The one I was telling you about last night."

"Oh."

I'd given it to her real slow and so it sounded good. I'd told her how I wanted to get on my own two feet and the battle I was having. I told her her old man might not like it—although I didn't say anything about the money angle, of course—and she said that we could get along even if he did get sore.

"I wish I had some money to put into it," Beverly said. "Like you asked me last night. It would make it so much easier."

"Yeah."

"But when you don't have it—you don't have it."

"I guess not."

We got up and I paid the check with some of her pappy's money.

"I wish there was a way of finding the money," she said, getting in the car. "I keep thinking there ought to be an answer."

I kidded her about using some of the money in her dad's agency for a little while, just to get her reaction.

"That wouldn't be right."

"No," I said. "That would be dishonest."

We rode along, the night deep and dark and damp around us. She dozed once in a while, curled up on the seat, and I had a chance to think things over clearly. Just being married to her made it seem a lot easier. I'd planted the need for money in her mind, set the stage for her reaction if I ever got nailed with the shortage. In a case like that she might stick to me and she might blow up with the suddenness of a five cent balloon. But, in any case, I had an excellent chance of riding out the storm—if it ever rolled up over Reagan's currency patch.

"Johnny?"

"Yeah."

"Turn on the radio."

"Okay."

After a while we were riding along to the tune of "Some-time, Somewhere."

"Love me, Johnny?"

"You know that, baby."

Sometime. Somewhere. Julie. Sometime. Julie. Somewhere. Julie. Julie!

"Always, Johnny?"

My vocal cords knotted up like a snake around a bush.

"Always."

She went back to sleep. I turned off the radio and listened to the soft top of the convertible bore through the wind.

It didn't have to last. I didn't have to stay married to her after things got leveled away. I could tell her it was over and just walk out. She didn't have anything to say about it. Not a thing.

The Ford plowed through the night, entering Pennsylvania, passing near the great steel works at Chester. A few flakes of snow whipped through the air and the road was icy in spots. I kept the car at fifty, driving steadily.

"Bet you thought I've been asleep, Johnny?"

"Yeah."

"Well, I haven't."

We rode along for another hour, not saying anything. Finally she moved across the seat and slid in close to me.

"There's something you ought to know, Johnny."

"Okay."

"I'm almost afraid to tell you."

"You don't have to be."

Maybe she was going to tell me she had twenty thousand dollars and that she'd lied about it in the first place.

"You can always tell me anything that comes in your head," I said.

Her hand fastened on my arm and her lips brushed my cheek.

"We're going to have a baby," she said.

"But, Beverly—"

"I just found out. I couldn't tell you before."

I felt like laughing. I'd been so smart, yes so damned smart, and all I'd done was beat her to the punch.

"That's great," I said. "Just great."

It was a lousy feeling, knowing that I'd just married her and that she was sitting there beside me getting bigger all the time. It was almost the same as buying a new car and, later, discovering that there was a big dent in one of the fenders. It made your head pound, made you want to puke—and you didn't know, not right then, what you could do about it.

"If anything," I said.

"What?"

"Hell," I said, dully watching the snow slap against the windshield. "I guess I don't know what I'm saying. It's got me all worked up. A kid? It's—well, you know."

I lit a cigarette and tried to think. She was right there close, her face upturned, her eyes studying me. I knew that she'd had this on her mind, trying to figure out how to say it. And now that it was said she was seeking assurance that it didn't matter.

"Johnny—"

"It's okay," I told her. "Don't worry about it."

I tried to imagine how it would be living with her and a kid. Perhaps it would be a boy and he'd cry a lot at first. But, then, he'd get older, growing up fast, and he'd talk to me and I'd wonder where he'd learned all the words. We might be out in the back yard, or down in the cellar or no place much in particular and he'd bump his arm and run, yelling, to his mother. I got that far with it before I could see his mother or hear her giving me hell because I'd been too rough with the little guy. Only it wasn't Beverly I saw. Maybe she was there, all right, but if she was I couldn't see her for the shadow of Julie Wilson's smile.

It seemed like a long time before we reached Waymart.

"I ought to stop off at the office," I told her. "You never can tell what's happened."

"Couldn't it wait until morning?"

I halted for the red light at the corner of Western and Orchard. Her chin was thrust forward stubbornly and I could see the shine of tears in the corners of her eyes.

"I'll only be a minute or so."

"That's all you think about, isn't it?"

"What?"

"Business."

I shrugged.

"You eat and sleep and drink it."

I shrugged again and parked the car at the curb.

"I won't be long, baby."

I started to get out but she got her arms around me and wouldn't let go. She crushed her lips to my mouth and her fingers dug deep into my neck.

"I'm an awful fool, Johnny."

"You shouldn't say that."

She buried her face against my shoulder and cried like I had belted her one in the jaw. I held her for a long time, trying to feel sorry for her and not finding a good reason. We'd had some fun before and we might have some again. She was going to have a kid because we hadn't waited. But now she was married and the kid would have a name. She didn't have a thing to cry about.

"Women are nuts," she said.

"Not all of them."

"Maybe it's just me, then."

"I wish I knew what you're bawling about," I said. "You give me the creeps."

"You wouldn't understand, Johnny."

"Not if you don't tell me, I won't."

"A woman thinks of her wedding night, Johnny." Her face was real close, her lips moving against my mouth. "She thinks of it as being—the first. Even if it isn't. Even if there's been lots of other men—including the man she marries—she forgets about them for that night. She goes to her marriage bed dressed in virgin white. And the next day she's really a married woman. If she's pregnant—that's all right. She's married. And—oh, God, Johnny!"

She didn't cry any more, just kissed me hard, her tongue sliding inside my mouth.

"That's why you wanted to stop at a tourist cabin?"

"Yes."

"Well, we can still do it."

Her hands came around front and moved inside my coat. I felt her fingers passing across the big hollow shell inside my chest.

"Thank you, Johnny."

I pushed the car door open.

"I'll be right back," I said.

"I'll be waiting for you."

I went to the front entrance and let myself in with the key. The elevator was on the bottom floor so I didn't have to wait for that. I just pressed the button, stepped in when the door opened, and rode on up.

There was a light burning by Janet's desk so I didn't bother turning on any others. A wire basket was partially filled with new applications. I grinned and started to whistle. That meant money for Johnny.

I put the applications aside and picked up a note from the middle of her desk. I read the note and stopped whistling. I almost stopped breathing.

4:45—Bank called. Account overdrawn sixty-four hundred dollars. Checks being returned tomorrow morning.

I took a couple of turns around the office and came back and read the note some more. It was like sitting in a graveyard reading the epitaph on your own tombstone.

"Son-of-a-bitch!"

Lately I hadn't done much of the banking but I'd kept a close check on the overall picture. While the account had never been flush there had always been enough on deposit to meet current expenses. I'd even planned on pulling out some of the money and siphoning it back into the Connors Agency.

I grabbed up a phone book. I wished to hell Janet had a phone in her place. But she didn't. She lived way out on the bus line, and she'd never had one put in.

I turned to the C section, trying to remember the name of one of the guys who worked in the bank. Crandall? Cranson? Crane? No, none of those. What was the matter with me? Couldn't I think? My finger stopped and moved back up the page. Crissman, Crissman. That was the name. Jeb Crissman. I must be going nuts, not to remember his name.

His phone rang and rang and after a while he answered sleepily.

"That you, Dick?" he wanted to know.

"No, this isn't Dick," I said. "This is Reagan, of Family Protective. I just got in, and—"

"Oh, yes, Mr. Reagan."

"—there's a note on my desk. Says we're overdrawn. I hate to bother you, but it's got me on edge. What's the story?"

"I guess it's true," he admitted. "There was some talk about it in the bank this afternoon. Just amongst the employees, you know. We'd never had any trouble with it before. It was—surprising."

"Yeah."

"But why don't you come down in the morning. Perhaps you can do something. The checks won't go back to Federal until eleven."

"I'd better do that."

"I suggest you do, Mr. Reagan."

"Sorry to have bothered you."

"That's all right."

He said goodnight and hung up. I glanced at my watch. Eleven-thirty. I started to swear. Less than twelve hours to mend the fence.

I sat down and tried to think it out. I'd never borrowed any money at the bank before but it would be worth a shot. As soon as I got those checks covered I could sit down and determine what had gone wrong. After that I'd have to spend more time around the office so I could be positive this same stupid thing didn't happen again.

I began to feel better.

All I had to do was show the bank how much business I had on the books and they'd know I was good for it. I could repay them in less than three months. Of course, that'd mean Connors would have to wait but I could worry about him later.

I took the elevator down to the first floor.

"What kept you so long?" Beverly wanted to know when I opened the car door.

I didn't know quite how to say it.

"Look," I said, trying to keep my voice level. "I hate like hell to do this, baby, but I've got to stick around here the rest of the night. There's some stuff I have to have ready by morning and it's going to take me hours to do it."

She just sat there numb, staring at me and saying nothing.

"You drive on home and I'll call you in the morning."

She moved in under the wheel, lips quivering.

"I'll make it up to you," I said.

"Johnny, you're lying!"

I felt like slapping her.

"You can't ever make it up to me," she said. "Not this night."

"I'll try."

She leaned forward and started the car. She didn't look at me again. I guess she knew how it was with us.

"I wonder," she said.

I watched the tail lights of the Ford crawl away through the falling snow. Then I went back into the building.

She was going to cry and sleep alone on her wedding night. That was tough.

I wished I could feel sorry for my brand new wife.

But I didn't.

CHAPTER XVII

The Crash

I SAT in the diner across the street from the bank, waiting for the doors to open. I'd been there since before eight.

"Hi, lover!"

I looked at the waitress. Every time she saw me in there she said the same thing. She was a little on the short side and she was all chest.

"That clock right?"

She nodded and pushed some fresh pies into the glass display case.

A couple of guys came along the street, carrying dinner pails. I wished that I was one of them. No worries. No real troubles. Just eight hours a day, a time clock to punch and a bill to pay once in a while.

"Hell," I said.

I pulled a sheet of paper out of my pocket and looked at it. I'd worked all night getting those figures. The bank was wrong. I was right. It was screwy.

When I looked up from the paper, across the street again, I saw that the bank doors had popped open.

"So long," I told the blimp behind the counter, and left.

I went up to the first window and told the girl what I thought of her bank.

"Perhaps you should see Mr. Gilson," she said, not at all ruffled. "Mr. Gilson will be able to straighten it out."

Mr. Gilson was a wiry little man in his early fifties and he didn't waste any time getting down to business. He led me into a tiny office, excused himself and returned a few minutes later and closed the door.

"These are our records," he said, dropping a fistful of yellow sheets on top of his desk. "Let's check them with yours."

"All I have written down here," I said, "are the deposits and the disbursements."

"I can't tell you much about the checks."

"But you can about the deposits? I know the checks are right."

"Yes," he said, getting down to work. "I can verify the deposits."

He worked steadily for about ten minutes. Every once in a while he'd glance at me and frown.

"Mr. Reagan," he said, pushing the papers aside, "I'm afraid I have some rather disturbing news for you. The deposit amounts which you have listed are, in most cases, incorrect. Permit me to show you."

He didn't have to be a math teacher to get the point across. The duplicate deposit slips I'd checked back in the office didn't mean a thing. She'd never made a full deposit; sometimes they were as much as two or three hundred dollars off.

I turned away from his moving pencil, cursing.

"Mr. Reagan," he said, "you've been duped."

"What?"

"Duped. Misled."

"Screwed," I corrected him.

A faint flush moved up above his white starched collar.

"Who is responsible?" he wanted to know.

I told him who she was and how I'd trusted her.

"I'll take a look and see if she has an account with us," he said.

He was gone quite a while and I kept thinking about her. How we'd slept together. What a damned miserable crook she'd turned out to be.

Gilson came back, rubbing his hands.

"She beat you to it, Mr. Reagan. Almost sixty-four hundred. She cleaned her account out yesterday."

I started to swear some more, then changed my mind. There was no use yelling about what I was going to do with her. She had me over a neat little briar patch and she knew it. I'd clobbered the money myself. I'd take care of her in my own way when I found her. With my hands. Alone. So that she'd not be so dumb the next time.

"Well," I said, "that doesn't take care of these checks."

Gilson nodded soberly.

"They'll go back if I don't cover them?"

He nodded again.

"I'm doing a good business," I said.

He shrugged.

"I've never borrowed any money before," I told him. "But if the bank could go along with a loan on this I'd be able to take care of it in a couple of months. After all, the business is there, it isn't as though—"

"I'm sorry, Mr. Reagan, but that wouldn't be possible. A loan of this size would have to be passed on by the board and there'd hardly be time before eleven o'clock. Even so—even though there was sufficient time—I'm sure they'd turn it down."

"Why?"

He went over and got the door open for me.

"I wish we could help," he said. "It isn't nice to turn people down. But we're very conservative here at this bank. We go in pretty strong for government bonds and real estate. A thing of your type—"

"Aw, nuts!"

I was still burning when I hit the street. That guy in there got five-six thousand a year to help people and all he could do was beat his gums and open doors.

I hailed a cab and jumped in. I gave him Janet's address.

"Make this just like New York," I told him. "Plow up the street."

"Okay."

It wasn't very far over to her place and he got me there in a hurry. I tipped him a couple of bucks and entered the brick apartment house. Her card was just above one of the mail boxes and it said 2C. I went up the stairs three at a time.

Her door was locked so I wore some of the varnish off it with my knuckles. All I got was an echo. I thought of going down to find the super but I had no idea where he might be. The door looked kind of flimsy and I decided to test it with my shoulder. On the third try the wood snapped and shuddered and I went through.

She hadn't moved out. Some books and things were lying around the living room and the bed in the bedroom had been slept in. Her clothes hung in the closets.

I went back out to the hall and met a guy coming up the stairs on a dead run. I handed him twenty as he was going by.

"Fix your door," I said.

He was still yelling when I got to the street but he didn't try to follow. I guess he'd figured he could fix the door for the twenty and have some left over for himself.

I walked back to the office, feeling the cold air and taking it easy. I was glad I hadn't found her in the apartment. Maybe it'd be just as well if I didn't find her for a day or so. She had a little neck, a real thin neck, and my hands kept going all the time like they wanted to make it smaller. She was a bitch. I'd been a fool. It was a bad combination.

I took the elevator up to the office and got out.

"Good morning, Johnny," Janet said.

She went ahead of me into my office. I closed the door and took off my coat. She sat down on the edge of the desk and watched me.

"I guess you wanted to see me," she said.

I slapped her hard, across the face. The red marks from my fingers spread from her temple down to her chin. With steady hands she lit a cigarette and blew the smoke in my face.

"What's bothering you, Johnny?"

"You know very well what's bothering me! You little crook! Cheap bitch! You swiped my dough. I want it back!"

I got some more of the smoke and it stung my eyes. I knocked the cigarette out of her hand and stepped on it.

"How's married life?" she wanted to know.

"Who told you that?"

She smiled and slid down from the desk.

"I tried to get in touch with you yesterday. Miss Noxon drove up from the city. I called over at Connors and they told me you were down in Maryland getting married." Her smile was contemptuous. "I only wondered how you liked it."

"It's none of your business."

"Okay."

"But I like it fine."

"I imagine."

She tried to get away but I grabbed her by the front of her dress and slammed her against the wall. She kicked me a couple of times but then I got my right knee in her belly and she started to cry.

"Where'd you put the dough, baby?"

She just shook her head.

"You're going to have trouble," I warned her. "A lot of trouble."

She bit her lower lip and kicked at me again.

"Go to hell," she said.

I ripped her dress all the way from the top to the bottom. I tore her brassiere loose and her breasts rose up, naked and angry, before me. I slapped her across the other side of the face. She whimpered and I shoved her into a corner.

"Get up the dough," I told her. "Before you part company with yourself."

She lifted her head and I could see the blood at the corners of her mouth. Her eyes were dry and fierce. The points of her breasts were like red lights in the early morning sun.

"You'll never get it," she said. "Not now. Not a stinking nickel."

"We'll see about that."

"It's mine, Johnny. I earned it."

"Are you nuts?"

"I earned it being your whore. Sleeping with you. Loving you. Getting pregnant for you." Her face twisted out of shape.

"Waiting for you," she whispered. "Waiting for Johnny the bastard."

"Shut up!"

"I won't shut up. It's true. The people where we rented know it's true. The hospital knows it. Surprised? You didn't know I had you down as the father, did you? And you paid the bill, Johnny. You didn't say anything about it at all."

"Slut!"

She pulled the rags in around her shoulders.

"I've been afraid for you, Johnny—for us. I knew you didn't have any money to start this business. I knew you stole it I didn't know how. All I knew was that you might get caught. I've been awfully afraid, Johnny!"

"You should've kept your nose in your own business, baby."

"I wanted to put it away like that to try and make you safe. Then yesterday—yesterday Miss Noxon came up here and said some awful things. I tried to reach you. And they said you were married. Married, Johnny!" Her voice broke. "You—damn you, Johnny!"

"That has nothing to do with my money."

Lightning flashed through the thunder clouds in her eyes.

"It's my money," she repeated. "You threw it away when you married her. It's all I've got left." Her laugh fell around the room like breaking glass. "I ought to get paid for all of the work I've done."

The buzzer sounded once on the desk and I picked up the phone.

"Hello."

"Johnny!" Beverly sounded excited. "Oh, darling I'm so sorry! Honest! I was an old meanie last night."

"That's okay."

"We'll make it up tonight."

"Sure."

Janet slid around the desk and grabbed up my coat. Before I realized what she was doing she had it on.

"Everything all right, Johnny?"

Janet went out and slammed the door.

"No!" I shouted. "The shingles are blowing off my roof. Call me back."

I hung up, cutting her off in the middle of a squeal. I ran to the door, jerked it open, and tore off toward the elevator. It was on its way down already.

I punched the button until my thumb got sore. Pretty soon the elevator started up and I stopped chewing my fingernails.

The elevator halted and the doors opened.

"Good morning," Cynthia Noxon said. "May I see you for a few minutes?"

"I'll be right back."

Her stare was cold.

"I'm sorry, Mr. Reagan, but I'm in a bit of a hurry."

I got the very definite impression that some of my luck was running at low tide.

"Well, okay."

"Over coffee? I haven't breakfasted yet."

"Suits me."

She didn't say anything more until we were seated in a booth, across from each other, in the restaurant down the street.

"Where were you yesterday, Mr. Reagan?"

"Getting married," I said.

Her smile was almost a sneer.

"Who was the lucky girl? Miss Connors?"

"Yeah."

"Well, isn't that sweet?"

I stirred my coffee, looking at her. There wasn't anything soft about her face; it had the hard veneer appearance of a mahogany table top. And her eyes had larceny in them, the kind of larceny that burns down inside of a person, scorching everything in sight.

"Look," I said, "I'm sorry about making you wait and all that. It was—one of those things. I wished to God I'd stayed here. Maybe I could have kept out of some trouble."

"And maybe you'd have gotten into it quicker," she said.

She was plenty touchy and I wasn't in any position to argue with her, so I let it go.

"This Janet," I said. "This Janet clipped me for over six thousand bucks. You know what that means? It means some of those last checks I sent you are going to bounce higher than a balloon in the wind."

Cynthia Noxon lit a cigarette and spit the smoke right at me.

"That makes my job a hell of a lot easier," she said.

I didn't have to ask her what she meant by that because all of a sudden I knew how the strings had been tied. She'd only been feeding me, sucking me in, and now that the melon was getting ripe she was going to cut it herself.

"What was your job?" I asked her, softly. "What were you going to do, Miss Cynthia Noxon?"

She spread her painted fingernails on the table top. She had nice hands. Long, slim hands. Hands that would strangle a guy at a moment's notice.

"I should have told you about our inspection," she said. "We put on general agents here and there and we have to check on every one of them."

"Go on."

"If we had signed up with the Connors Agency that would be a different thing. But we didn't. We signed with you. Johnny Reagan. Johnny Reagan who's a nobody."

"Thanks."

"You didn't pass our inspection, Mr. Reagan."

"Get to the point, baby."

"That's all," she said. "I'm giving you thirty days notice of voiding your contract and then we take over."

She tried to get up and leave the booth but she didn't have a chance. I grabbed hold of her hands, hurting her, and then I slid around the table and moved in beside her. She started to yell but I slapped one hand across her mouth and jammed her head into the corner, tight against the wall and the end of the booth.

"Listen to me, you dirty bitch!" I told her. "I know what you're doing. You're moving in because of all those renewals I've built up. I won't get a nickel. You'll get the whole works."

She fastened her white teeth into my fingers and I took my hand loose. I could see that she wasn't going to do any yelling. We both looked down at my hand and watched the blood drip onto the top of the table.

"You're awfully smart," she sneered. "You ought to be an insurance man."

"There's just one thing I want to tell you," I said. "You're going to regret this caper for a long time to come."

"In six months you'll be out of the seat of your pants," she told me. "You'll be busted and you'll be in trouble with the bonding company. They'll own every nickel you make for the rest of your life."

"Keep spinning the wheel, baby."

She pushed out against me and I didn't try to fight her any more. A lot of the coffee club had drifted into the restaurant, yelling and making wise remarks. There was no use arguing with her about it. She owned the scissors and she could cut up our contract any time she felt like it.

"You never had a lousy dime that belonged to you," she said. "We checked you good and you always owed somebody—a finance company, or a store for a suit, or something like that. Then all of a sudden you get a big chance with this Connors outfit and you break out with a lot of cash. Enough to start an agency of your own." She paused and pushed against me some more. "Enough so I know you're a louse, Johnny Reagan."

I let her go and she didn't waste much of her time getting up.

"Thank you, Mr. Reagan," she said.

I sat down and ordered some more coffee. But I didn't drink it. I just sat there swearing and hating them all. It was funny, but I wasn't so mad at Cynthia Noxon. That was her business, getting other people to be dumb and staying smart herself. All the time I'd been doing it so smart I'd been so dumb I should have drowned myself. But that Janet was quite another angle. She'd twisted me out of shape until I was bent double and still going further. She'd been my girl and I'd tried to make it up to her and she'd turned out to be a pirate.

I paid my check, went out to the street and down to a bar a couple of doors away. I sat down and began to play tag with Old Grand-Dad. And I began to get sore all over again.

They were all in the same class, the three of them. Cynthia and Janet and Beverly. They all spelled money troubles. Two were crooks and the other was too dumb to have any money.

I had two more quick jolts.

There was Julie, only Julie, and now she probably wouldn't touch me with a five foot stick. I'd gone into Connors deep and hard and now these dames were throwing the dirt in the hole, covering me up.

The guy behind the bar ran out of Old Grand-Dad so I switched to scotch. I put the first one away, neat, and my brain rolled over on its side. The bartender poured another and some of it slipped out of my mouth and ran down my chin. I pulled my knees up and pressed them in against the bar, hoping that would help me to stay aloft of a stool that changed sizes every once in a while.

"You don't want any more, Mac."

"Shut up, damn it, and get to work."

"Okay, okay."

I kept on drinking and thinking of just one thing. Everything else was scrambled up and hazy but I was real clear on that one. I had to beat them.

And I knew how.

CHAPTER XVIII

Caught Short

THE DAYS of the next month twisted together like a cob web. Cynthia Noxon was the spider and I was the fly. I kept running around that web, studying the angles. And when I moved in I tore the web wide open.

It wasn't easy.

"I wish you'd stay home once in a while," Beverly complained. "You're never here. You're always on the run."

"A couple of weeks more, and it'll be all over."

"I wonder."

We were living in her parent's town house, rattling around in those big rooms like dice in a wooden box.

"You'll see, baby. Just wait."

"I'm waiting."

There was always something tense between us. Maybe it was the result of that first night when I'd had to leave her. I'd tried to make it up to her, bringing her flowers and candy and stuff like that. Sometimes she seemed to act the part of a wife. Sometimes she didn't. I didn't worry about it. I was only passing by her corner, anyway.

"You're a great one," she'd say. "You marry me and then you don't show again for three days afterward."

"I guess I got a snoot full. I never got married before."

"Just enjoyed all the privileges."

That's the way it would start. She'd remind me of the night on the raft, and of other nights, and she'd say I'd only wanted one thing and now I was sorry I'd ever got it. She didn't get any argument from me on that. When I didn't say anything she'd go on raving about the kid and how her friends would count backwards on their fingers after it was born. She told me that she'd written to her father and mother about the marriage and that the first letter she'd received from them afterwards had been filled with good wishes. But the next letter had been short and curt. They'd said they wouldn't bother writing again. The old guy was getting up and around and as soon as he could travel they were going to fly back. That one bothered me. It was the same as sitting in a card game opposite a dealer from hell. You either took the pot or you crapped out.

After three weeks I was ready to make a play for the pot.

The day I signed the deal with the Provider Insurance Company I sat down in the office all alone and laughed. I was laughing at Connors and his pregnant daughter—I was laughing at Janet and the two days I'd spent looking for her—and I was laughing at Cynthia Noxon and the way she'd come back to me, later, with her skirt under her arm.

They could all go pound sand.

The guys in the office didn't like it when I cut out the radio program. That is, they didn't like it at first. But when I told them how it would work, how they could knock their old customers off again right and left, they went all out for it.

It was just as simple as tying a noose around somebody else's neck. The Provider Insurance Company was a little old outfit located in central New York State. It was chartered by the state, it had plenty of contracts to sell, but it was dying up there because nobody knew what they were doing. They grabbed for my idea like sharks after a corpse.

They had a clip policy called The Provider, a real dilly that sold for eighteen dollars the first year and fifteen the second year. It didn't pay for a thing but it was put up on good quality paper and it looked as straight as a lifetime contract with one of the big outfits. It was easy for my agents to call back on their old clients, tell them they could save money and get something better. In less than a week I knew it would be a smasher.

Several times I went around looking for Janet but she had packed in and nobody had heard from her. Once, I found a letter from a dress house in her mail box and three days later it was still there. I gave up going around. But I didn't give up thinking about her.

I could see myself lifting six grand and hitting the high road. I'd been brought up to take what I wanted and pay it back when I felt it wouldn't bother me any. But Janet was different. She'd seemed straight to the point of being pathetic. I couldn't figure her. She was a dame and I was stuck.

Cynthia Noxon called me twice during that month. The first time to sneer and the next time to sneer again.

"You have everything mailed down here before your time's up," she said. "Don't try any schemes with me, Johnny Reagan. I'll beat you every time."

"You'd think I didn't know that already," I said passively. "You'll get them even if I have to crawl down there with them on my back."

She hung up, laughing. Then I laughed. I laughed so hard I thought my head would break. Just wait until she began mailing out those renewal notices and she got lapses instead of dollars! The little bitch!

I spent a few bucks and got a report on Family Protective. It was what I wanted to see. The company had been going good at first but now it was listing the other way. No reason was given for this but it didn't matter. All I needed to know was that she would be hurt if her gold mine in the hills turned out to be lead.

She was going to find tough digging.

Occasionally I'd stop around to the restaurant to see Julie but I didn't work overtime at it. The word had drifted back from Waymart about the agency and she'd heard the worst of it.

"Let it die," I told her one night. "I'm trying to promote my way out of it."

She leaned across the counter, her mouth round and her eyes careful.

"Honest?"

"Yeah. I'm sick of running my legs off. I just want to cash this mess in and settle down to some real living."

A customer drifted in and she went down to wait on him. He was one of those kind who reads the menu as though it's a full length novel. I glanced at the clock and saw that it was close to seven. I'd told Beverly that I'd be home to eat around six-thirty and by this time she'd probably be ripping up the floors with her hands.

"Take it easy, Johnny."

I stopped by the door.

"Okay."

She poured a glass of water and stopped to pick up my dime by the register.

"I hope it works out for you, Johnny."

"So do I."

"You've gotta think of your wife, Johnny."

I went out and closed the door. She always had to prod the sore open and watch the blood run.

It was a warm night and I drove across town through the slush. I parked the car alongside the house and got out in water half-way to my knees. I swore and went up the steps to the back porch and into the kitchen.

She sat at the kitchen table drinking coffee. She hardly looked up when I entered.

"Hi, Beverly!"

There was a moment's silence.

"Why don't you wipe your feet?" she wanted to know.

I stared at the floor. All I could see were a couple of spots of water.

"I guess I forgot."

"You forget a lot of things."

I took off my coat and carried it into the closet. When I came back to the kitchen she was washing her cup in the sink.

"What's for chow?"

She looked at me steadily.

"Nothing."

"Oh."

I went to the refrigerator and pulled the door open. I got out some lettuce and cold cuts and threw a sandwich together. The coffee in the pot was old and lukewarm but I poured it into a cup and sat down at the table.

"I have news for you," she said, slowly drying her hand on a towel. "Big news."

"Okay."

"I was to the doctor today. He says it'll be a seven months baby."

I didn't try to figure the exact time but that sounded pretty close.

"Well," I said, "you won't get so big that way."

She slapped me in the face with the towel and walked on through to the living room. I ate the rest of my sandwich and finished my coffee. Then I followed her into the dark room. She was lying on one of the davenports bawling her head off. I turned on a light, picked up the evening paper and sat down.

"I guess your nerves are all shot to hell," I told her. "You're blowing fuses right and left."

She sat up and wiped the tears out of her eyes. I could see the bulge of her belly real plain and her face was getting fuller.

"I have some other news for you," she said.

"I'm listening."

"Dad and mother will be home in less than three weeks."

"You heard from them?"

"How else would I know?"

I grunted and studied the sports page. I read about Durocher and his next year's Giants and I wondered if I could crawl out from under before Connors got back. It was short notice for the twelve thousand bucks I still owed, but maybe it could be done. Four thousand a week. Eight hundred every working day.

"You'd better get yourself another job, Johnny."

The way she said it, plain and simple, I knew she wasn't just batting words around. I tossed the paper aside and lit a Camel. Then I leaned forward, my elbows on my knees.

"Baby," I said, "you and I had better have a talk."

She started to cry again.

"You're so miserable, Johnny. So terribly miserable!"

"Thanks."

"You've ruined—everything."

"Stop blaming me all the time."

"All right, why shouldn't I? You don't care about me, do you?" Her mouth twisted as though I'd slapped her. "Do you?"

"I don't know why you say that, baby."

"Baby! Baby!" She got up and wandered around the room. She moved with her back straight, her long neck rigid, her face lifted high. "Don't you know any other name except 'Baby'?"

"Well, for—"

"I always hated it. Hated it, do you hear!" She swung around suddenly. Round beads of sweat clung to her forehead. "Sometimes I even think I hate you."

"So do I," I said. "I'm sure you do."

She didn't move when I went over to her. She just stood there waiting, her lips tight and her eyes dull.

"I want to know what happened," I said. "Somebody pulled a string some place. You weren't like this before."

She nodded solemnly.

"Who's been peddling tales? You don't want to believe everything you hear."

"Even from your own father?"

I had my hands on her shoulders but she shrugged them off. She went over and stood at the window looking out. It was one of those mild winter nights when the snow melts on the roof and you can hear it dripping from the eaves outside. The kind of a dark uncertain night that makes you feel all alone and very far away.

"Give me the rest of it, Beverly—straight."

"He called me this afternoon. He was—upset. He said he was coming home as soon as he could. He said he was going to let you go."

"Is that all?"

"My God, isn't that enough? Your own father-in-law—"

"Skip the romance and give me the rest of it."

"He said he had a letter from somebody—about you. He wouldn't say who wrote to him, but—"

"The stinking little bitch!"

"Johnny!"

It wasn't enough that she'd nicked me for six grand, she had to keep right on short-circuiting everything I tried to do.

"Give me the rest of it, baby! All of it!"

"That's all—what more could there be? He's going to have auditors in—oh, it's awful! Just awful!"

"Yeah."

I wished that I was back in the box factory, hammering boards and yelling at the hump-backed foreman. I wished that I was almost any place except where I was.

"I didn't quite believe him, Johnny. I stopped down to his office this afternoon. They all hate you down there."

"Sure. They're jealous. They think I spend all my time sitting in some bar. They stink."

"They know about that thing over in Waymart, Johnny. And they wonder."

"Yeah."

"It's dishonest, Johnny. Dishonest."

"To hell with them!"

She moved away from the window and across the room. She still held her head high and proud but her shoulders pulled down like they had heavy weights on them.

"You don't love me, do you?"

She had all the words there this time. I could feel them rolling up and choking in her throat and burning her mouth. Her eyes were dry and glistening at the same time. I thought about her father and three weeks and I thought a lot about what she'd just told me. Somehow, I knew that she had to know and I had to tell her.

"No," I said. "I don't."

"Thanks for being honest about that, at least," she said, her voice half a whisper.

"Okay."

"You don't feel anything, do you?"

I shrugged.

"You just think it's finished?"

"I guess that's the way it is."

"Well, guess again, Johnny."

"You name it."

She came toward me slowly. She didn't seem to be crying but there were tears rolling down her cheeks. Her breasts were full and pulsing and I could see the gentle roll of her swollen stomach.

"Don't worry," she said, whacking me across the face, "I'll name it."

I rubbed the spot where her fingers had struck. I knew that she had cut me with one of her fingernails because I could feel the blood, soft and warm and sticky.

"You're going to stay married to me, Johnny Reagan. Don't ever think you're going to walk out and leave me high up on a stump."

"Now you're talking like a slut."

"You taught me," she said and let me have it again, but not so hard this time. "And you're going to teach me something else, too. You're going to teach me that you've got some guts and that you can live with someone you don't even like. You're going to live with me and support me, Johnny, for a long while. You're going to give our kid a name and watch him grow up—even if it kills you."

I didn't say anything. She was right. I'd used her—or thought I had—and now I didn't want her any more. She had every good reason to be plenty sore. Only she wasn't very smart. She didn't know me. I wasn't buying anything I didn't need.

"We're going to get an apartment," she said acidly. "And you're going to live in it with me. If you don't, you'll not only have trouble with dad at the office when he gets back but I'll also have charges filed against you for rape."

"What!"

"You heard me, Johnny dear. Rape. It's a nasty word and they'll never believe it. But I'll drive you down in the gutter so far you'll never crawl out."

I could see her, then, this wife I had married. She was rich and I was poor but we had one thing in common. Neither one of us wanted to lose anything. But one of us would. Plenty.

"I believe you would," I told her.

"Try me!" she taunted.

I needed three weeks, maybe four, and it would all be over. One way or another it would end. Either Connors would move fast enough to clip me for borrowing some of his dough or I'd be sitting in a spot where I could throw a harpoon and catch Cynthia Noxon in a very sensitive area. I needed those three weeks and I had to buy them at any price.

I got my wife in my arms and started paying the price.

She yelled a little at first and she told me not to but after a while she didn't fight so hard. I kissed her and she kissed me back and she kept whispering in my ear how sorry she was she'd been so rotten.

"Kiss me again, baby," I said and turned out the light.

"I'm too heavy to carry," she said.

"I'm a big boy, honey."

I carried her all the way upstairs and into the bedroom. We stood by the bed and I helped her undress. Her lips were hot against my neck and her hands wouldn't leave me alone.

"Men are so lucky," she said.

"I don't know why."

"I'll show you why," she whispered.

And then we were together on the bed, two twisted bodies offering each other nothing except the pleasures of the flesh.

Maybe it didn't even amount to that.

CHAPTER XIX

Jingle Bells

HIS NAME was Goldstein and he had a junky little store down on William Street. He'd been there for thirty years, selling anything he could get his hands on, and the place was littered with the stuff he hadn't been able to sell.

"I don't know why you don't set fire to it and jump out the door," I said, laughing.

That's another thing you learn in the insurance business—some people you can kid with, putting them at ease, and others have to be played straight and stiff. This Goldstein was one of those who could be kidded into a corner. He had a kind, round face and bent shoulders. For all of his business years his gray eyes were innocent and steady.

"Sometimes I feel like it," he admitted, absently pawing through a tin box filled with rusty bolts and nuts and screws. "Honest, I must have a million bolts around here some place that'll fit that door knob, but I've looked every day for a week and I haven't been able to find one yet."

"Maybe you should buy a new lock," I said.

"That's an idea. I've got some locks around here, too."

I'd had him figured at the proper angle, all right. Around sixty, easy going and as tight as the skin on a hundred dollar bill. The estate notice in the paper had said that he was inheriting around fifteen thousand from a sister and it had struck me good right off. Only I wasn't after the whole fifteen—just part of it. And part meant half.

"It's tough to invest a dollar these days and make a buck," I told him. "All you do is sharecrop with the government."

He grunted and played with the nuts and bolts some more. The way he had his head turned sideways I could tell that he was thinking. I'd been in there talking to him about twenty minutes and he knew who I was. I hadn't said anything about the inheritance, only pointed out that he was a businessman and that he might be considering an outside investment.

"I wish I knew who sent you," he said after a bit.

"Well, I couldn't do that, Mr. Goldstein. As I said, a mutual friend suggested that I stop around. Maybe you've told him something about your plans and maybe you haven't. In any case, he wouldn't want you to feel that he in any way is betraying a confidence. You know how it is."

He nodded and pushed the bolts aside. He took out a handkerchief, wiped off his hands and put on a pair of five-and-dime glasses.

"It's got to be a good investment," he said. "You've got to show me."

"Glad to."

I didn't have a rate book with me and I didn't take the trouble to ask him his age. A life annuity with an insurance company, if properly presented and explained, looks about as attractive to an active businessman as a woman without her teeth. I just got out paper and pencil, wrote down seven thousand five hundred dollars and told him he could get a hundred bucks a month for life. I gave it to him fast and short so he could get it real clear.

"A lot more than the building and loans," he said presently, studying the figures.

"A lot more than anybody."

Hell, I wasn't kidding him.

"And you get it every month?"

"Sure."

"For how long?"

"Till the day you die."

"And—after that?"

"What's left, plus interest, goes to anybody you might name."

"Hm," he said, thinking about it some more and, "Hm," again. Then he looked me straight in the eye and asked, "How do I know this is on the level? It sounds so good—"

"Are you familiar with the Connors Insurance Agency, Mr. Goldstein?"

"Why, yes, I guess so. They're downtown, aren't they?"

"Over the building and loan."

"Yes, I know about them. Big outfit."

"Well, I'm the manager down there."

"Oh?"

"Here's my card. If you want, why don't you call them and ask?"

It would be perfectly all right if he called because they'd just tell him who I was and let it go at that. Maybe nobody down there thought I was God's gift to the insurance world, but they wouldn't do anything to hurt the business.

"Oh, well," he said, "what would you lie about it for?"

He was asking me.

"Suit yourself," I told him. "I've told you what it is and what you can do. Maybe you don't have the money. That's not my business. All I do is tell you what we have and you can make up your own mind."

He pulled the tin box over in front of him again but I knew that he wasn't looking at the bolts and nuts and screws. He was picking them up and dropping them like they were fat five dollar bills. I could see by the twist of his mouth that I had him dancing on the end of a string.

"When would I get my first check?"

"A week from today."

"As soon as that?"

"Sure."

"And it's a hundred dollars a month? Every month?"

"Right! No vacations for us."

"For as long as I live?"

"Even if you last to a hundred and fifty."

We talked some more about it and I kept on building him up to a point where he could hardly see straight. He said something about the door being left unlocked when we went out but I told him I'd drive him down to the bank, and back, and that we wouldn't be gone long. We weren't. He drew the money out of his account in a matter of minutes and I made par for the course getting it away from him. A half hour later I let him off in front of his shop and he thanked me for having stopped around. I thanked him and got out of there.

I'd given him a receipt and he'd favored me with seventy-five hundred bucks.

I guess both of us were happy.

On the way across town I stopped in at the Pig and Whistle and hoisted a couple of fast ones. Outside it had started to snow again and the juke box over in the corner kept playing "White Christmas."

Merry Christmas! Happy New Year!

I had a couple more just for the hell of it. An elderly woman came through, collecting for the Salvation Army. I gave her a buck and told her to keep her hand out of the kettle. She told me to go to hell and tossed the dollar on the bar. I pushed it toward the bartender and kept on drinking.

The damn world was growing up fast. I had over seven thousand in my pocket and a couple of rabbits by the neck. One of the rabbits was Connors and the other was Cynthia Noxon. Connors could go crawl into his hole. With Cynthia, I might even follow her into the nest.

"Got your Christmas shopping done?" the bartender wanted to know.

"Yeah."

"Stuff's high as hell, ain't it?"

"I wouldn't know," I said. "I didn't buy anything."

He went down the bar and started talking to somebody else. I guess he thought I was drunk. I wasn't. I was thinking so much I didn't have time to get a load on.

Christmas presents? Who the hell could I make happy under the Christmas tree? Beverly? We were still living together, up there in her old man's house, but we weren't working at it any more. The morning after the night we'd had the big row she'd blown her whistle again. She called me an animal and a couple of other things you only learn by reading Freud in a dark corner. I made up my mind she had some sort of a sex complex, like sex guilt or something similar, and I'd gone in for sleeping alone.

To hell with her.

Merry Christmas!

Maybe I should get a present for Janet. Yeah, that would be a scorcher. I'd get a gun, or a rope, and I'd put a great big card on it. One edged in black. And I'd write something on the card, like "Baby, swing yourself over a limb in a high wind," or "Give yourself another hole in the head." I laughed and the bartender's look didn't bother me a bit. Where the hell would I send her present? The little bitch was running with my dough—running light and free while I sat in a bar knocking my brains out.

And, then, I began to get just a little drunk.

I kept thinking about the hotel, where we'd met, and of that first night when she'd cried and became a woman. And, later, when we had an apartment and she'd ask me if we were going to get married. Stuff like that. And when she'd left me, wanting to forget, saying it was the right thing to do. The chills she used to give me when she thought she was pregnant and the end of it there in the hospital, without any money, waiting for me to pay the bill. Then, after that, the job she'd done for me at Waymart, looking sharp all the time and plenty distant, only to stab me at the earliest chance. Damn her!

"Another," I told the bartender. "Keep 'em running."

"Okay."

Sure, I'd send her a card. I'd write her a poem about how she looked that morning in my office, her clothes half ripped off, six thousand bucks richer because she'd thrown a hoop over my bank account.

"Fill it up."

"Take it easy, Mac."

"I am."

So she was gone and I couldn't do anything about it. I couldn't go to the cops and say they had to do something because she'd stolen some money from me that I'd stolen from somebody else. I couldn't do a damn thing about it except shut my mouth and hate her.

Merry Christmas!

Skoal, you drunken bum.

Maybe I should get a present for Julie—Julie, who hopped tables and who still lived on Clarke Street. Julie, with a bastard kid and the principle of a choir singer. Julie, who put a price on everything a few years late. Julie, the girl I had to leave alone.

"One for the road, mister."

"Okay, Mac."

One for the road and one for the woman I loved. Why couldn't it have been different? Physically I was years away from Clarke Street, yet mentally I still sat right in the middle of it. Scheming. Ducking. Hoping. It was no different than lifting stuff off the five-and-ten counters or swiping fruit from the corner stand—except that the stakes were bigger, the profits bigger, the worries bigger.

"Another, Mister."

"You sure as hell ain't gonna make that road, Mac."

"Who's apt to move it?"

"I dunno, but it won't be where you left it."

"This one's on Goldstein," I said.

He looked at the empty stools on either side of me.

"That the friend with you, Mac?"

"Sure."

He was still looking at the stools when the redhead came in and sat down on my right. She'd already hung up her coat and I got a pretty good look at her. Without the paint her face would have busted the mirror back of the bar, but the rest of her was all woman. She smiled and put up the for sale sign. She smiled again. Cheap.

"Maybe you're not so drunk at that," the bartender said.

I had the drink on Goldstein.

Merry Christmas, sucker.

Only he wasn't a sucker. Nothing was going to happen to his money. I'd use it for a while, maybe six or eight weeks, and then I'd take it back to him. I'd tell him that the company called the deal off, but the two payments he'd already received he could consider a bonus. It wouldn't take me longer than that, no more than two months. With this seventy-five hundred plus the earnings of my office in Waymart I could put every-thing square with Connors. Twelve thousand! Brother, that was a lot of money. But it could be done. The old boy might know something had happened but he'd never know what it was.

"To Goldy," I stated and rolled another one down.

Two months left of running dead ahead on a one way track. Then Goldstein would have his money in his pocket and I'd be clean. That ought to be about the time Cynthia Noxon would start crying that she was starving to death on lapses. Maybe I'd be able to sell her my agency in Waymart—sell her what she had stolen from me.

"This is the last one," I told the bartender. "And fix one for Red."

Yeah, I'd sell to Cynthia Noxon all right. For money. And something else. Something that ought to be strictly in her class.

"Thanks, mister."

"Okay, Red."

"How'd you know my name?"

I cocked my head and looked at her. Those lips were full and crimson and her eyes were as wild as the night. The lights from the back bar lit up her hair like a rocket.

She got up and moved her stool closer. When she sat down again she put one knee right up against my thigh and left it there.

"Lonesome, honey?"

"What do you think?"

Her left hand slid down and touched my leg. With her right hand she lifted her glass and drank, her stare never moving away from my face.

"It's almost Christmas," she said.

I grinned and spun a half dollar on the bar.

"Jingle bells, jingle bells—"

"Shut up!" she said. "I'm going to cry."

I stopped singing so she didn't bother to cry. She finished her drink. Her hand kept moving around on my leg.

"I've got to run up to the place and see how my mother is," she whispered. "Want to come along?"

"What for?"

"Are you kidding?"

I bought us another round and thought about it. A chippie. A real chippie. Just like the rest of them. Only she was honest. She had something to sell and you could either take it or leave it.

"What do you do for a living, mister?"

"I'm a farmer."

She took my right hand in hers and turned it over, looking at it.

"You're a liar," she said. Her eyes were blue and steady. "I'll bet there's only one thing you ever farmed."

"Yeah?"

"Let's have another drink."

"When you going up to your place?"

"Right after this one."

"Okay."

She didn't fool around with the drink like I expected. She put it away fast and stood up. After she got her coat from the rack I held it for her and she shrugged into it. For some reason I thought about that coat of mine Janet had worn out of the office, covering her nakedness. I wondered if I'd ever get it back. I decided I wouldn't.

We went out to the street and I told her I had a car and we could ride. She said, no, it was only a couple of doors away and we'd walk.

She was wrong. It was the third door.

"Look, mister," she said, after we got inside the warm hall. "I've got to level with you. I hate this!"

"You don't live here."

"No. The man works nights. He never gets back until after eleven and—well, it's all right. We can go under the stairs—there's an opening there—and if we keep quiet—"

"Merry Christmas," I said.

"What?"

"I said, Merry Christmas."

She was silent for a moment and I could hear her breathing hard there in the darkness.

"You knew," she said. "You saw the line."

"Yeah. On your finger. Real white, like you'd just taken the ring off."

"I did, if it's any satisfaction to you."

"Maybe it's easier that way."

"What do you care?"

"I don't know."

I had a loose twenty in my right hand pants pocket and I wound my fingers around that.

"You got somebody?" I wanted to know.

"Kids. Two. A boy and a girl."

"And the old man?"

"It's none of your business."

"I know it."

"Korea," she said, wearily. "Dead—six months, almost. And they got his insurance all screwed up. They write me I'll get it all at one time. What the hell good does that do?"

I went over to the door and opened it. I took out my wallet and found another twenty and a ten. Then I closed the door and stuffed the three bills into her cold hand.

"Merry Christmas," I said and kissed her once.

"Merry Christmas," she said and cried.

Then I left her and went out into the street and pulled the door shut.

A sign in a store window said there were four shopping days left before the big day. I laughed and walked on. I didn't have to worry about that.

She could do it for herself.

CHAPTER XX

Christmas Eve

I SHOULD HAVE gone home but it was too early for that. Beverly would be horsing around with the Christmas presents, wrapping them up, and she'd have the radio turned down low with the music soft. If I wanted to be entertained I'd have to sit in a corner, away from the tears in her eyes, and scratch my head with first one hand and then the other.

Merry Christmas, baby. To hell with you. Spook around the house all the time, growing bigger every hour, and squall all you want. To hell with you.

I got in the car and sat there watching the people in the street, under the green and red lights, walking with packages. Some of them had kids and some of them were alone and some of them walked so close together that you knew they weren't just thinking about Christmas. They were thinking about that diamond ring, and the monthly payments, and how the jeweler could have the ring back if that wouldn't do the trick.

Rings, I thought, what was so important about a ring? A guy bought one, stuck it on a girl's finger, and then asked her if it was all right. Maybe she was coy or a little afraid or a whole lot of both and she'd tell him they ought to wait. The guy would wait, feeling sick, and he'd wonder if he should have bought her a bigger ring, if that would have made it easier and sooner. Sometimes the guy would look around and he'd find another girl who didn't need a ring, didn't need anything at all except a little time. And maybe the girl would do some looking, too, and she'd stumble into a guy who didn't have to give her a ring, a guy who wouldn't take up a lot of her time.

What'y know, I thought, I must be getting slopped. I rolled down the window and let the cold air sweep inside. Then I started the car and pulled out into the traffic.

Merry Christmas, you stupid jerk.

Half-way down the block I parked in front of a liquor store, got out and went inside.

"Merry Christmas," the clerk told me.

He looked like a patsy if I'd ever seen one.

"Sure," I said. "And, now, little man, what would you like Santa Claus to bring you?"

"Say, mister, you don't have to get that way."

"Shut up and give me a bottle of Old Forester."

"Okay, okay."

I left him a ten and carried the bottle out to the car. I sat in there, watching the people again, and worked the cap loose. Usually I didn't drink liquor but once in a while it does a guy good to change his style. The door on the sidewalk side of the car was jerked open.

"Hey, how about a slug of that, bub?"

I looked at the face, a middle-aged face with a week's growth of whiskers and deep lines. His eyes were those of a man who walks a crowded street alone.

"Sure," I said and handed him the bottle.

He took a long drink. His hands shook and some of it ran down and dribbled off his chin.

"Thanks, mister," he said, returning the jug.

"Don't mention it."

He hesitated before closing the door.

"You're a good guy," he said.

That made one.

I wiped off the top of the bottle and had a couple of snorts. The liquor was hot and it burned going down. I capped up the bottle and put it on the seat beside me. I had a feeling I was going to get lit up like a rocket on Fourth of July.

I drove down the street, wondering what I ought to do. If I knew where Janet was I'd hunt her down and twist her arm until she unhooked herself from that dough. But I didn't know. Maybe I'd never know.

There were plenty of places outside of town where a guy could have fun. This time of the year there'd only be the loose ones floating around, the guys and dolls who wanted to whoop it up, the unhappy creatures who either didn't have a home or didn't want to go there.

Like me.

I drove real slow, swiping another belt of Old Forester. Hell, I shouldn't be unhappy. Maybe I was in for a tight squeeze in the next couple or three weeks, but after that I'd have the good old world by the short stuff. It wasn't like other years when I'd bought cheap wine and mixed it with beer for kicks, just because the rooms at home were so messed up I didn't want to hang around there.

I could remember my mother, when I'd been a kid, and how she hadn't been able to make cookies or fruit cake and how she'd cried and cursed at the old man about it. The old man,

I guess, figured the holidays as open season and he wound up every year in a series of blind staggers. One Christmas Eve he'd lugged home a pig's head, tossed it on the kitchen table and told her to start making sausage. She'd flown into a rage, cursing him, and she'd gone off to bed. The next morning he'd been asleep at the table, using the pig's head for a pillow.

I circled the block, still wondering what I ought to do. If it hadn't been so far I'd have driven over to Waymart and looked up that Trail of the Lonesome Pine singer. But it wasn't worth the effort. She interested me just about as much as a dead policy holder.

It was only a short distance to Clarke Street and I headed that way. I guess that's where I'd been going in the first place, only I'd, been putting it off, kicking myself around.

Merry Christmas!

There's something about the end of the year, the phony forgiveness that a lot of people like to hand out, that sort of gets you. You get to thinking about that night when a lot of guys around you crapped out, when the mail didn't come, when your first sergeant shot himself because he was sick and tired of it all. You think of the little blonde who lifted the twenty off the bar and did a Houdini through the girl's room. You think of snow on the ground, of red-faced people plodding through the night and singing, and you remember how it had been for you when you were a kid and you sat in the dark and cried because there wasn't anything at all. You keep thinking like that and drinking and the whole world suddenly seems sort of small and sad.

You wish it was the second of January. Or April Fool's day. Or almost any time except what it is.

I parked in front of Julie's house, on the opposite side of the street, and put the bottle back into action. There was a light in her window, a Christmas wreath with a red candle in the center of it, and I could see other lights beyond that. Small lights, all different colors, the kind they put on trees. Once in a while somebody walked in front of the tree lights, blotting them out, and I knew that it was Julie.

I got out of the car and started across the street. But I didn't go all the way. I just stopped and looked. She was in there and I wanted to be with her, but I knew that it wouldn't be any good. She had the tree and her kid and she'd be thinking, maybe, about that lousy sergeant and the way he'd left her, alone, to pay the consequences of their fun. As soon as I got my boat bailed out I'd come back and take her for a ride, just like I'd told her. A long ride. One that would last us for a spell.

There was still some liquor left so I had a real long one as soon as I crawled into the car. Then I drove on down the street and parked. Not in front of the house, but a few doors away. There were several old junks bumper to bumper in front and I knew that my brothers and their families were tearing things apart upstairs.

I walked back to the house and up onto the porch. I could hear them all right. And they weren't singing. They were fighting like a bunch of pack rats in a dump.

"Hello, Johnny."

I looked down to the end of the porch, into the shadows. She was leaning up against a post, smoking. I walked on down to her.

"Hi, Lili."

"Your family's really raising hell up there," she said.

"Yeah."

"You going up?"

I thought about that, trying to flush the whiskey out of my brain so I could figure it out.

"To hell with it," I said.

If I took the money up to my mother now they'd only get it away from her. They'd drink it up and when it was all over nobody would have anything left except the shakes.

"I'm glad, Johnny."

"You're welcome."

She hunched her shoulders, pulling the coat in close. She flipped the cigarette into the yard and stood looking up at the sky.

"It's beautiful, isn't it?"

The clouds under the moon looked gray and ugly and lonesome.

"Yeah," I said.

She moved around a little bit and when she finally stopped she was right up against me. The perfume back of her ears crept up over the collar of the coat and slapped me in the face.

"Christmas is a hell of a time of the year, Johnny."

I agreed that it was.

"It's the one day that when you're no good you know it. You think of all of the things you've shoved aside and you want to slit your throat."

"I'll loan you a knife," I told her. "I'll even watch you do it."

She was just a chippie and I had half a snootful and I didn't give a damn about her.

"Must you be so cruel?" she wanted to know. She didn't move away from me but she started to tremble and I could hear her crying. "Can't you be human with me for once?"

"All right. I'm sorry."

"You sound it."

"Say, what do you want me to do, get it engraved on a twenty dollar bill for you?"

"Now you're being nasty."

"Have it your way."

She tilted her head further back, resting it against my chest and she stopped crying. The moon hammered its way through the clouds and the whole night lit up.

"Let's go inside," she said suddenly. "I'll buy you a holiday drink."

I didn't say anything. I could hear the racket upstairs and I thought of my wife at home and of Julie down the street.

"There's something I want to tell you, first," she said, turning around. "You're all wrong about your father. He's just an— old fool. It was never him, Johnny. Never. And there isn't going to be anybody else after tonight, not for a long time."

"How often do you tell yourself that, Lili?"

Her face looked sad.

"Every Christmas," she said.

She pulled my head down and touched her lips against my mouth. They started to move, opening up, and I could feel the hot flash of her tongue.

"Come on," she whispered. "Let's go."

I went.

She had bourbon, without ice, and some ginger ale that was as flat as yesterday's beer. I wished that I'd brought in the Old Forester but I was too tired to go out and get it. Besides, there couldn't be very much left.

"Fix yourself another one if you want," she yelled from the bedroom. "I'll be right out."

I poured a long jolt into the glass and went over and sat down on the davenport. I could hear the Reagans upstairs cutting the night apart. Once in a while I thought I could hear my mother swear, but I couldn't be sure. My old man was laughing all the time and some of the kids were crying.

Lili came out of the bedroom wearing one of those shortie nightgowns that no woman in her right mind would put on unless she had a sheet to go with it. There was just one light burning in the room, a table lamp with a weak bulb and a red shade, but I could see her fine. I could see so much of her as she came across toward me, cat fashion, that even the liquor I was drinking lost its jounce.

"I wish you'd put something on," I told her.

She stood in front of me, right up close, smiling.

"I'd only have to take it off again," she said.

I tried to look away from her but I couldn't. I had no business being in there with her and I ought to get up and leave. She was a real pro, a flesh merchant, and I didn't have to live out the rest of the night this way.

"So long," I said.

I got up, spilling the drink, and started for the door. She let out a half strangled cry and grabbed me, hard. I tried to shake her off but she came in, pressing tight.

"You're a hell of a Santa Claus," she said.

My hands were on her shoulders, digging in. She moaned with the pain and jerked away. One of my hands slid down to where it shouldn't go. I stopped hurting her then and she stopped moaning and there were just the sounds of our hard breathing in the room.

"Turn off the light," she said.

I went over and turned off the light.

The liquor snarled in my brain and my eyes hurt as I stumbled to the davenport. She was there waiting for me. Her hands were warm and soft and she wasn't at all afraid.

"Neither one of us is any good," she said huskily.

"No."

"Then we don't have a thing to lose."

Her arms went around my neck, pulling me down there beside her. Her mouth was wild and alive and she bit me once or twice. My hands touched her and the fire fled through her, growing bigger all the time, until it shot up into a sheet of flame that pulled the night apart.

"Johnny!"

"Damn you," I said.

The night belonged to us.

CHAPTER XXI

Homecoming

OLD MAN CONNORS and his wife hauled back into town the day after New Year's. I was at the office in Waymart, trying to get rid of a hangover, when Beverly phoned me the news.

"They're here in the apartment," she said. "Dad said he'd like to see you right away."

"Okay."

"And—Johnny, let's not make it too miserable, huh?"

"No."

"I'll have Martha fix dinner."

"All right."

I hung up and took an aspirin. It was a day off and nobody else was working. I'd driven over only to get the telegram. I'd have driven any place to get that thing. I'd been waiting long enough for it.

I read it again.

Mr. John Reagan

Provider Insurance Company, Waymart, New York

Suggest you call me New York office immediately relative ending personal feud.

Cynthia Noxon

I read it some more. I looked for a drink but there wasn't any, so I sat down and laughed without it. Little Miss Money-maker herself crawling like a snake in the hot sun. I picked up the phone and asked for her New York number. I sat back, feeling good, waiting for the kill.

"Hello," she said.

The way she said it—no zip to it, just dead, like so many words written on a graveyard wall—I knew that she'd been sitting there alone, waiting, chewing her fingernails off up to the knuckles.

"Well, bless your lovely thieving heart!" I told her. "Happy New Year!"

"I was sure it was you," she said, some of the deadness going out of her voice. Then, "Hello, Johnny Reagan."

"Hello, yourself."

"You got my wire, then?"

"Look," I said, "I'm paying for this call. Sure, I got your wire. You think I call up every jerk I know just for practice? Don't give me any romance, baby. Just tell me what you want. Maybe I'll listen and maybe I won't. I get tired of listening real quick, these days."

"Always the cocky, Johnny Reagan."

I put my feet up on the desk and waited. I could afford to wait.

"Know something, Johnny?"

"What?"

"You're plenty smart."

"Thanks."

"I thought we might be able to work out a deal, something reasonable and profitable for both of us. I don't mind saying that you've cut deep into us, Johnny. Real deep. And I'd like to remind you there's a law against doing it the way you've done it. Encouraging people to give up their insurance. In case you don't know, the insurance department says you can't do that."

"Well, write them, baby. Don't tell me."

"You know I couldn't do that."

"Of course I know it," I told her, grinning. "You do the same thing all the time, so what would you want to get yourself in trouble for? The only thing is I've got you stopped on rates and you can't do a thing about it. You know you can't, so why don't you just forget it?"

"I wish I could," she said slowly. "I wish I could tell you to go—but I can't. You know I can't. We've stretched out far down here, Johnny. Bigger offices, more space, more of everything."

"That's smart. Now you can starve in luxury."

"It isn't very funny."

"I don't think so either." I took my feet down from the desk and leaned forward, cupping the phone in my hands, my fingers curling hard around it, almost wishing that the black rubber was her smooth neck. "I never thought it was funny, baby. You tried to break me in the lousiest way possible. You've done it to others and you figured you could do it to me. You made your plans on doing it. And you lost, because I don't whip easy. Why don't you admit it?"

"What do you think I'm doing?" she demanded angrily. "I'm asking that we throw in together. We'd make a good team, Johnny."

"Yeah," I said. "With you at bat all the time and me out on a slide in to home? No, thanks, baby. My back's too broad. You couldn't miss."

"Or I could buy you out," she suggested quietly.

"If you had the money."

"I might be able to get it—for that."

"My price is high, baby."

"What do you think I'm paying now?"

I knew, then, that I had her. She had to have my renewals to back her up and she'd do almost anything to get them. If she could do that she could arrange to have her Family Protective premiums reduced and in this way she could, eventually, assume the accounts from The Provider.

"I'll have to think about it," I said. "Maybe I'll buy you out."

"Please, Johnny!"

"Well, you've got to give me some time. Say, until the end of next week?"

"I'll drive up."

"Hell, I don't care what you do."

I hung up and let her say good-bye to herself. Another week or so over the fire wouldn't do her any harm. She'd be plenty hot by that time.

I put on my coat, locked up and rode the elevator downstairs. It was cold outside and the sky was leaden gray. I didn't care much if it snowed. It could snow so hard it got to be nine feet on the level. In a couple or three weeks I'd have my carcass stretched out on a sand pile at some beach in Florida. Maybe I'd be alone and maybe I wouldn't.

I drove toward home, thinking about Connors and his wife and Beverly.

Just a couple of days before, Beverly and I had moved into a four-room furnished apartment on Hillcrest Avenue. It was plenty ritzy and cost one twenty-five a month. There were thick rugs, colored drapes and modern furniture that'd break your back in two sittings. I'd felt about as much at home in that place as I'd have felt in an overturned barrel in the middle of the town square. The day after we moved in Beverly had a couple of pains. The doctor said she ought to take it easy, just lie around and do nothing, otherwise the baby might come too early. That deal was going to cost me another two hundred a month because I'd had to hire Martha, a fat young kid who had two children by a runaway husband and both eyes fastened on an easy buck. For a guy who wanted to live it was like getting nailed up to a cross.

When I got to town I stopped at a drugstore, bought a pack of Camels and had a Coke. I wasn't in any hurry. I hung around there maybe fifteen minutes, listening to some young guys argue about a hot rod they were building, and then I decided I might as well go along and get it done with.

They were sitting in the living room, lapping up the last of the coffee, when I breezed in. The way Beverly said hello you'd think it was putting a lot of wear and tear on her span of life. She just sprawled out in one of the chairs, giving everybody a good chance to see what was bothering her. She hadn't put on any make-up and she looked so white you'd think she was bleeding to death. I got the impression that she'd known they were coming.

"Welcome, home," I said.

Her old lady nodded and went back to staring at her toes. I couldn't blame her. She had feet big enough for a guy in the infantry.

"Nice place you've got," Connors said as I put my coat in the closet.

"Yeah."

He'd lost some weight but other than that he looked about the same.

"We got tired of waiting for you," Beverly said. "We already had dinner."

"Okay."

"Martha's got stuff in the kitchen."

"I'll get something later."

"Suit yourself."

"Don't worry," I said. "I will."

The old lady jerked her head up and Connors scowled and chewed on his cigar. I guess they could feel the tension, the rising force that was always there between us. She'd throw face powder all over the bathroom and then she'd scream at me because I used too much coffee in the morning, or not enough, or that I should go to a restaurant and not make it at all. She was wound up all the time like a big spring in a tiny box.

"We've got to get the house opened up," Connors told me. "I'll bet it's cold over there."

"It must be."

"Maybe we ought to put up at the hotel tonight."

"Maybe you had, at that."

He was just making conversation, killing time, trying to find a spot where he could move in.

"I guess you wanted to talk to me," I said.

"Well—yes."

"Then let's get going with it."

He glanced from his wife to his daughter, then to me and around the circle again.

"It can wait until we get down to the office tomorrow, Johnny. I don't want to drag the women—"

"We can go in the bedroom," I said. "Or up on the roof. It won't take any longer now than it will later."

"You listen to Dad!" Beverly told me, sitting up straight. "If he tells you—"

"Shut up, baby!"

There was a shocked silence.

"Well, of all the toughs!" Mrs. Connors exploded, her thin face getting red. "Young man—"

"Look, Mommy," I said, pushing the bedroom door open, "these are my marbles and I'll pick them up when I feel like it. Your old man has something on his mind, he should get it off." I gave Connors a nod. "Okay, Dad, let's go to confession."

He came on in and I closed the door. His face was white and mad. I motioned for him to sit on the bed but he shook his head and kept standing. I went over and leaned against the dresser and lit a cigarette.

"You got something to say," I told him, "say it."

I was fairly sure he had it figured that I'd crawl for my job and yell for another chance. He had it figured wrong.

"I didn't know you folks were going to have a family," he said. "I just didn't know it."

"That's one thing I don't have to prove."

"I was—surprised."

"Maybe I wasn't."

He took out a fresh cigar and stuck it in his mouth. Some of the anger had left his face but I could feel the bitterness in his eyes as he looked directly at me. And it was in his voice, too, crowding up fast and choking him.

"If it wasn't for Beverly, Johnny, I'd—I'd—"

"Don't let that bother you," I said. "You don't have to fire me. I quit. When you get in the office tomorrow, look in the upper left hand drawer of your desk and you'll find my resignation."

I could see that I was taking it all away from him. He'd come back boiling mad and now I was giving him just what he wanted even before he could ask for it.

"I want you to have an audit," I went on. "Get yourself a good CPA in there and tear those records apart. Then I want you to put on a piece of paper that they're okay. That's all I ask."

A CPA or any other accountant who could add would find those big deposits and they'd wonder about it. Twelve thousand bucks in three weeks! But they wouldn't be able to prove anything and the overall picture would come out right. I was as safe as cash in the bank.

"I wasn't going to fire you," Connors said, staring at his fat hands. "When I found out about the baby I changed my mind. For her sake, Johnny—not yours."

"I don't want anything," I said. "You can stick it."

"She'd be better off if she left you."

"I hope you can talk her into it."

"Johnny!"

"You creeps give me a pain!" I wandered around the room, smoking furiously on the cigarette. "You think I like this setup?" I demanded hotly. "You blowing a spoke, or something?"

"Beverly's in a delicate condition," he said. "We ought to let all of this go until later."

"That's got nothing to do with it."

"She ought to be in a rest home, Johnny. You should have made arrangements for her to go someplace where she wouldn't have to do anything."

"She don't do anything around here," I said.

"That isn't the point. It's the mental strain. It's easy to see you two don't get along."

"You're really clever, Pop."

"I don't know what it is."

"Well, I do."

"I don't think I want to know, Johnny."

It was a good thing he didn't, because he wasn't going to get told by me. Thinking back, remembering all of it, it was easy to understand that she'd married me because she didn't have much choice. We'd been sleeping around together and when the inevitable happened there wasn't anything else she could do about it. But after we were married she must have started looking for something else other than safety and she hadn't been able to find it. I didn't love her and she probably felt only shame everytime I came near her or whenever she thought about it. And I guess maybe I felt shame, too—or, at least, I felt something hollow and hopeless in my stomach that threatened to make me very sick.

"I don't like to rush you," I said, "but I've got to get back to work. If there isn't any more, let's knock it off."

He walked in silence to the door.

"There isn't any more," he said.

We went out into the living room. Beverly was crying and her mother was shouting and they were having a hell of a good time.

"Maybe you people want to fight in private," I said.

Her mother glared at me.

"I think you've done enough," she said. "Why don't you just go on out and leave us alone?"

"Where?"

"Any place. Only don't come back."

"You telling me to get out?"

"I don't think I have to write it out for you," she said. "You're no good for Beverly."

Connors plopped down into a chair and stared moodily at the floor.

"I wish to God we could stop arguing," he said. "I get myself all worked up and my heart starts thumping around."

"Then you keep out of it," his wife said. "You don't even have to listen."

"He'll need cotton," I told her. "It'll take a yard of it for each ear."

I was looking at the old lady so I didn't see Beverly get up from the chair. I didn't even hear her moving around. The only thing I heard was the coffee cup break when she rapped me across the back of the head with it. It didn't hurt very much and it didn't make me mad. I just knew that it was the end of something or other, and whatever it might be was okay by me.

"I'm going with them," Beverly said. "It'll be better that way."

The cold grounds from the coffee dripped down my back. I scratched my skull and tried to stop it from itching.

"Yeah," I said.

"Don't get any ideas about a divorce," she said. "This is your baby and it's mine and you're going to support it. You're going to support it every day that it lives and breathes. I'm going to see that you keep remembering this for a long, long time to come."

I didn't give her any argument on that. I knew the kid was mine. I'd never told her it wasn't, or thought that way, either. The kid would be mine, as much as hers, and I'd take care of it for as long as I walked, or swore, or drank. Maybe it was a lousy way to put it, even in my own mind, but when a guy stopped doing those things he just stopped all the way. And that's how long I'd take care of that kid.

Beverly went into the bedroom and got her things together. After a while her old lady went in and helped her and I could hear them talking like crazy. Connors sat in the chair staring at me. He looked away when I found a bottle in the closet and put aboard a couple ounces of cheer.

None of them bothered to say good-bye or so long or go to hell. They just gathered her stuff under their arms and took off. I guess every window in the building rattled when Beverly slammed the door.

"Happy New Year," I said to nobody in particular.

I thought about calling a lawyer to find out about a divorce but I decided to shave instead. There was plenty of time to take care of that later.

And, besides, maybe something else might happen.

CHAPTER XXII

Stillborn

SATURDAY I moved out of the apartment and checked into a hotel room in Waymart. I was working over there all the time anyway, so it didn't make sense to drive back and forth just for the privilege of rattling around in four rooms.

"You all by yourself?" the bell boy wanted to know.

"I don't see anybody else, son."

"They should've given you a single, mister."

I looked at the wide double bed and gave him a wink.

"Forget it. Something like this is great in an emergency."

He snickered, pocketed the buck and left.

I spent maybe an hour unpacking and getting things put away. By the time I finished it was almost four. Too late to go back to the office. And I'd had enough of it for one week, anyway. There was just one thing I had to do yet and that was the biggest of all. I'd kept it until last because I had to be sure of where I was going. Now that I knew that, now that I was certain about how it would turn out, there was no point in waiting longer.

I changed into a sharp gray suit, put on my dark blue overcoat and left the hotel. The car was in a parking lot, so I walked down there, tipped the kid a half and got the Ford rolling.

I wondered how she'd act, how she'd see it, and if it'd be the way she wanted it, too. Of course, I wasn't free yet, I was still married to Beverly, but the lawyer had told me it shouldn't be difficult to get a divorce. After all, she'd walked out on me and I'd stayed right there for a couple of days, waiting for her to return. The only thing the lawyer suggested was that I wait until after the baby was born. He said if we did that I could go into court and say how I wanted to support the kid and it would look better all around. As for the rape business, that didn't amount to much, since she couldn't prove anything and she'd lived with me as a wife for quite a while afterwards. If Beverly wouldn't see things my way I might have to go to some other state but that wasn't important because I intended to take a trip anyhow. One way or another, though, I'd get the divorce and that was all what counted.

When I reached town I drove right to the restaurant and parked. The shadows of an early evening hung low and it was getting much colder outside. I kicked the door open and went in.

The little guy in whites who usually sat at a rear table was behind the counter. He wiped his hands on his apron and came over as I sat down.

"Coffee?"

"Where's the girl?" I wanted to know. "Julie Wilson. She working?"

"Who the hell knows?" he demanded, watching the door. "She never show up."

"Not today?"

"Not two days. The boss he get sore. I get sore—plenty. She do this last week, too."

"That's funny."

"Not funny," he said. "I work butt off."

That's tough, I thought. Two, three months ago you were sitting in a pile of junk on the other side and now you're too damned lazy to breathe.

"Thanks," I said.

I went out and got into the car. I felt as though something had been cut loose inside. I was a jerk. I was completely gone on a dame and I had to do something about it.

I drove down to Main and turned right. The Saturday night crowd was boiling over the sidewalks. I took it easy until I got to South Street and then I cut off to the right. I could swing around that way and stay out of the traffic.

At the next block I went left again and picked up speed. But when I rolled up to the first intersection my foot just slid off the gas pedal. It's funny how some things strike you, rolling right up out of the past and smacking at you deep inside. Like that old brick house on the corner, the one without any lights, where I'd followed Janet up the stairs one night a long time ago.

It all came back then, just for a second, the hotel and walking down here and how warm it had been. The darkness of the hall, too, and the sweet taste of her lips, and her scared and excited breathing when we'd gone into the room.

I cursed silently and felt the tires spin on the ice. It was all over—the apartment and the hospital and the six thousand bucks. It was finished. She'd been smart and I'd been a chump. So what?

About a mile further down I drifted over to Main and parked near the corner of Clarke Street. I sat there for quite a while, listening to the kids squeal as they played in the snow, wondering what I'd say to her. It was a waste of time.

I got out and walked around the corner, looking down the street, moving slow. Some place down there in the darkness was the house where my folks lived and where I had lived. I speculated, vaguely, about what they might have done with the hundred I'd sent them at Christmas. Probably the old lady had bought herself another set of false teeth and the old man had gone on a howling drunk. Some day, when I had the time, I'd go down there and find out.

I went up the steps and across the porch. The frost in the boards snarled with the cold. From inside came the muted sounds of a radio. I pushed on into the hall and found the door to her apartment. I knocked and waited. I knocked and waited some more. Then, suddenly, the radio came up real loud and the door jumped open a foot.

"Hello, Julie."

She was wearing a red robe that wasn't tied too securely and her hair was all mixed up around her face.

"Hi ya, Johnny."

Her eyes were animal and shiny and I got the odor of liquor on her breath. I glanced down the break in her robe, past the white fullness on one partially exposed breast. The ragged ends of a nightgown hung below the robe and I could see her bare feet and I could smell the sweat all around her. I wanted to get sick right there in that hall.

I kicked the door open. "I been down to the restaurant, looking all over—"

I stopped talking. I stopped walking. For a second or so I thought I'd stop living. I was conscious of the dim lights, of the door being closed—and of him.

"Well, Sammy," I said.

"What's new, Johnny?"

He was stretched out on the old sofa and he didn't have a damn thing on except a pair of shorts. A bottle of liquor sat on the floor and a couple of half filled glasses beside it.

"Sammy Grick," I said, my voice tight.

It was as simple as drawing a straight line, but I'd had no way of knowing about it. She'd met him in the office, up there at the Connors Agency, and some of it hadn't worn off.

"What are you trying to celebrate?" I asked her. "Next Christmas?"

She walked around the room, holding the robe tight, every bit of her moving in all directions at once.

"You ought to know," she said.

"Maybe."

Sammy sat up and lit a cigarette. He held out the pack but I shook my head and he put it away again.

"Connors get in touch with you?"

"When?"

"Today."

"No."

Sammy started to get up but changed his mind. His shorts didn't fit him so good.

"The old guy was calling my place early this morning. Wanted to know where he could reach you."

I'd spent the night in Waymart and it'd only taken me a few minutes to move out of the apartment.

"To hell with him," I said. "I got no time for that guy."

A grin twisted Sammy's lips.

"You got any time for your wife?"

"Just what do you mean by that?"

"She's in the hospital." He let me wait while he finished his drink. "They took her down there about five this morning. I guess she was pretty bad. The old man sounded all busted up. He thought you ought to know."

"Thanks."

"You don't sound worked up about it."

"I don't even know what's bothering her," I said. "Maybe she's just tired."

But I didn't feel that way about it at all. I was going around inside like a butter churn. She was my wife and I'd lived with her and now there was something wrong. She'd been all mixed up and unhappy for a long time and she hadn't ought to have anything else happen.

"So long, kids," I said and walked to the door.

"Johnny!"

I gave her the same look as I'd give a Hudson County prostitute.

"So long, baby."

"Johnny!"

She jerked my hand away from the door and slammed it shut. Her eyes were all wet and the tears hung like big drops of rain on her cheeks. She crawled in close to me, putting her head on my chest, and I could feel the warmth of her.

"Don't go," she pleaded. "It's a trap. They want to arrest you."

"You should stop drinking so much."

"Please, Johnny!"

I pushed her away. She tripped on a rug and almost fell. The robe flopped open and for a couple of seconds she was practically naked. Very deliberately she took the sash and tied it tight, staring at me all the time, her mouth pulled out of shape.

"Go ahead," she said. "Maybe you deserve it, lying to me the way you did."

Off and on I'd told so many lies that I couldn't remember them all.

"I didn't lie to you, baby."

"You said you were going to get everything straightened out. That day down in the restaurant you told me to wait and that you'd do what's right. You're a damned liar, Johnny."

I shrugged and opened the door again.

"They've got the auditors down there and Mr. Connors is going to get you at last. Twenty thousand dollars you're short, Johnny!" Her voice rose up into a sob. "Oh, Johnny, why did you do it?"

Very slowly, very carefully I closed the door. There was a key in the lock and I turned that and dropped it into my pocket.

"You'd better get on your feet, Sammy," I said.

I could see it all, like it was a picture smeared on the wall. He'd been after her, chasing her, wanting her. And she'd tried to stick to me and believe. So he'd lied about the audit, making her hate me, driving her to him.

"Tell me how short I am," I said, moving toward him.

"Johnny!"

"Tell me!"

He slid along the davenport, trying to get away. I jumped fast and grabbed. I caught the loose flesh on his chest in my left hand, locked the fingers shut and twisted. His face got red and he let out a moan. I jerked him upright and slammed my right into his jaw. Blood and saliva spurted from his mouth and I could see the corner of a broken tooth. I let go of him and fired another right. His head snapped back first, going all the way back, and then his body went with it, moving up over the davenport and pounding into the wall.

"Now you've got something to play around with," I told her. "Fix him up so he'll run again."

"Johnny!"

I unlocked the door.

"Johnny!"

She was still yelling my name when I reached the sidewalk, but by the time I got to the corner the wind whipped it away into the night.

I got into the car, trying not to think about it, and started the motor.

I drove down Main to Crawford and took the traffic circle up over the railroad. There were two hospitals in town but the big one, St. Francis, was the most popular.

The Catholic Sister behind the desk at St. Francis told me Beverly's room number. A nurse took me up to the second floor in a slow-moving, ether-scented elevator. I walked down the hall and quietly went into her private room without knocking.

She was lying there, her face almost as colorless as the white sheet, staring vacantly at the ceiling. At my entrance she turned her head slightly, then quickly glanced away.

"Hello, Beverly."

She was silent for a long, agonizing moment.

"What do you want?" she whispered.

I went and stood beside the bed.

"Nothing. I just heard you were here."

"Is that all you heard?"

"Yes."

Her shoulders rose and fell sharply.

"He's dead," she said. "He was born dead. A month too early, the doctor said. Too much excitement."

I felt like getting down on my knees and telling her what a no-good bastard I was. For a couple of seconds I felt empty and torn and broken inside. I knew then that I'd wanted the kid to live, no matter who his mother was, as long as he was part of me.

"That's lousy," I said.

"You didn't want him."

"That isn't the way I feel right now."

"It's the way you felt before, Johnny."

"Maybe," I admitted. "And maybe I didn't know just how I felt."

There was a long, awkward silence. I started to light a cigarette, noticed the No Smoking sign and put the cigarette away again. I took a gum wrapper from my pocket, found it minus the gum and stood there holding it. I bent down and sniffed the flowers on the side table.

"He wasn't even old enough to have a funeral," she said. "Isn't that awful?"

I nodded. She stirred in the bed and I could feel her looking at me.

"Just a name," she said. "You can give them a name if you want to. Any name. Just as long as you don't want to use it again."

I straightened slowly. She was blinking her eyes, driving back the tears.

"I called him Johnny," she said. "Johnny Reagan."

"Yeah."

"I'll never want to use that name again."

"No."

She pushed the sheet away. She raised one hand and found my arm. Her fingers were strong and warm.

"I've done a lot of growing up in here, Johnny. My mother wondered why I didn't cry a lot. I couldn't cry for him, Johnny. I didn't do it. You didn't do it. It happened. God did it."

"Maybe."

"He hates us, Johnny.'

"That's a rough thing to say."

"I don't mean as individuals." Her voice was growing steadier, softer. "I mean as two people who did some awful things together and even worse things to each other."

"I see what you mean."

"And if he had lived—well, it would have gone on. I don't mean we would have lived together, or stayed married, or even seen much of each other. But you'd have come to see him, sometimes, and he'd have been there, living, not letting it die for us."

"You hadn't ought to think about it so much."

"I just wanted to tell you."

"All right."

Her lips trembled and her eyes brimmed full.

"I think I loved you once, Johnny," she said. "It'll never be the same with anybody else, ever again."

I was pretty sure she'd outgrow me fast, but I didn't say anything.

"You're so big," she said. "So cruel. So absolutely ruthless. I—I feel so helpless around you."

She'd had me a little mixed up, too.

"I'll see you later," I said. "Some day when you're feeling better, when we can talk."

Gently I freed her hand and let it drop to the bed. I bent and kissed her briefly on the mouth.

"Dad's very upset," she said. "He told me you weren't short."

I nodded and walked to the door.

"Forget it," I said. "I'll drop around in a week or so." I thought about Florida and the hot sands and what I was going to do. "Or I'll write," I added. "I might write, anyway."

"Johnny?"

"Yes, Beverly."

"I won't be home, Johnny. And you won't have to write, or see me. I'll get the divorce."

I hesitated only a moment.

"Okay," I said.

I went out into the hall and closed the door. The elevator was on its way down and almost as soon as I jammed the button the doors opened and I got on.

The nurse had to remind me to get off when we reached the main floor.

I even forgot to ask them if I was supposed to pay the bill.

CHAPTER XXIII

Sold

ON MONDAY morning I had a short note from Cynthia Noxon telling me she'd be up later that day. The envelope had been originally addressed to me at the Connors Agency but somebody over there had been kind enough to forward it to Waymart. It wasn't a challenge and it wasn't an admission of defeat. She just said she was coming.

"When this tomato shows up," I told the dumpy girl in the outer office, "have her cool her buttons out here for a spell."

"Yes, Mr. Reagan."

I went back and gloated over the renewal file. It was thick and bulky and loaded with money. And she'd pay for every nickel of it. One way or another. Or both.

At ten the phone rang and somebody yelled in that it was for me.

It was Connors.

"I have to see you, Johnny. Right away. Can you drive over?"

He sounded pretty urgent but I didn't let that annoy me.

"Not today," I said. "I'm wrapped up like a mummy."

"Well, listen to this, then. You'll be interested in this, Johnny. I no more than got into the office this morning when a man showed up. He was looking for you."

There was a brief pause.

"Yeah?" I could feel it coming, something wrong, sweeping in and over me. "What did this guy want?"

"His name is Goldstein, Johnny. He wants to buy another annuity just like the one you sold him." Connors' voice dripped disgust. "Remember that one, Johnny?"

Nuts, I thought, I should have given the old guy the works. He'd had fifteen thousand and I'd only tried for half because I hadn't wanted to frighten him off. Now he was crossing me up. He thought he had a real bargain and he was going after the rest of it. What a laugh!

"Sure, I remember him," I said, thinking fast. "I've been trying to broker that thing all over the place, only I haven't had any luck."

"We sell annuities," he reminded me quietly. "Maybe the income isn't as high—or fantastic—but we sell them."

"Look, I just figured that thing wrong, that's all. I was figuring ten when I should only have used seventy-five hundred. I didn't want to disappoint him. I've been trying to work it out."

"I'll bet."

"I'll have it all squared away this week."

"You'd better, Johnny." His voice became suddenly sore and vicious, ripping at me across the line. "You have that money in my office tomorrow morning or I'm turning the whole thing over to the insurance department. I told Mr. Goldstein that I'd be responsible—you used my name and you were in my employ at that time—and I will. Only you won't get away with it, Johnny. You took that money from him and you either have it some place—or you don't have it. And you'd better have it. I'm telling you, Johnny. Don't play it out any longer."

The telephone whanged in my ear and I jumped about two feet. I sat there staring at it.

A couple of hours later I was over being mad. I almost thought I might be getting a little bit scared. Old Connors had meant it about the insurance department. They could move in and throw me in jail or do almost anything else they felt like doing.

Things, it seemed, were rolling up a short, dead-end street.

I didn't go out for lunch; I just sat on my nerves and waited. I wondered if Cynthia Noxon would show, if she'd have any money and, if she did, what I'd be able to work out with her.

I got out those renewals and looked at them again. All told they were worth somewhere around forty thousand dollars but I could never hope to get that much for them. Maybe half. I was counting on half, which would give me enough to pay off Goldstein—I'd been going to do that, anyway—and I'd have plenty left over to make a big splash some place else.

The hands of the clock moved around to three. I could feel the sweat running down my sides and legs. I kept going to the door and looking out front to see if she was there. All I got was more suspense.

About quarter of four, when I glanced out, I hit the jack-pot. She'd just come in with some elderly-appearing guy. I didn't keep her waiting.

"Hi, there!" I said. "Come on in."

She said something to the guy and he sat down in a chair like a trained dog. Then she came through to my office, wrapped in a three-quarter fur coat, her hard, cosmetic face in first class shape, her eyes bright and washing all over me.

"Gee, it's good to see you!" she said.

She was lying but I grinned and closed the door. I waved her into a chair alongside the desk. She opened the coat and sat down. I got a flash of white flesh as she crossed one leg over the other.

"How have you been, Johnny?"

"Fine."

"Still going strong?"

"Yeah. You know me, baby."

I dug out a bottle and offered her a drink. She said she didn't want any, thanks, but I didn't let that stop me. I had one for luck.

"Who's the money bags out front?"

She flushed slightly.

"Did anybody ever tell you that you're very crude?"

"Not lately."

"He's—well, he's an associate."

"I see."

"You make it sound so nasty."

I winked at her and lit a Camel. Now that she was in the office with me, where we could talk and I could see her, I wasn't so nervous. I tried to stop thinking about Goldstein and his stinking money. I couldn't let her know, not for a second, that I had to sell and had to sell fast.

"Things have been a little rough on you, huh?"

"You know that, Johnny."

"Well, you brought it on yourself, baby. You dropped the egg out of the basket and it hatched."

"We all make mistakes."

"Sure."

"One of mine was misjudging you."

She uncrossed her legs and I got an even better look.

"I came up to talk terms," she said, leaning forward. Her dress dipped low in front but I couldn't see anything except a handful of pink silk. "I'm prepared to be reasonable, Johnny."

"You're the one that's buying."

"Or selling," she said earnestly. "One of us has to move over. We can't go on fighting each other. It doesn't make sense."

"No."

"Name your choice, Johnny. Do you want me—or do I get you?"

I let my eyes wander over her body.

"Who wouldn't want you?" I inquired.

"You know what I mean."

"Yeah—I do and I don't. You haven't got anything to sell, baby. Why should I pay out good money for your crummy outfit when I can steal every bit of your business and it won't cost me a thing?"

"You have a point there."

"I guess I have."

"So it would seem that I'm the buyer, Johnny. Let's see your contract."

I pulled it out of a drawer and tossed it into her lap. It was a simple agreement, straight to the roots of the matter and not spoiled with a lot of legal hedges. It gave me the right to sell my business to any licensed agency at any sum which I might be able to get.

"That part's all right," she said after a while.

"It's a little different than the kind of stuff that you hand out."

"You should always read what you sign, Johnny."

"I'll have to remember that."

"Now—how much are your renewals?"

"You ought to know," I said. "I swiped them from you."

"I know it's quite a lot."

"Forty thousand."

"That sounds about right." She crossed her legs again, more carefully this time. "And how much do you want for them?"

"Twenty," I said. "Cash."

She took a deep breath and it hung there in the silence. I guess it was about what she expected me to say.

"That's quite a lot, Johnny."

"Take it or leave it, baby."

She got up and draped her coat over the back of the chair. Then she walked around the room, slowly, her arms folded across her breasts. She stopped at the window and stood looking down at the street for a long time. Then she turned around, still standing the same way, and I knew something was wrong. Her red lips curled away from her teeth and it wasn't a smile at all. It was a sneer and the hate in it flared up into her eyes, freezing deep into the pupils.

"I'll give you five," she said.

I jammed the cigarette into an ash tray. Some of the hot end stuck to one finger, burning, but I didn't pay any attention to that.

"Go to hell," I said.

She began walking around the office again, every line of her body swaying.

"You're a sucker," she said. "I'm doing you a favor by giving you that much."

"Don't be so generous, baby. You might overdo it."

She drifted over and stopped in front of me. She held her head up high and proud and the sardonic twist still spoiled her mouth.

"After all," she said, "you only need seventy-five hundred. If I give you five you ought to be able to make it. You should get about a thousand for your car and—"

"What!"

"You heard me, Johnny boy. I dropped in at the Connors Agency on the way up—thought you might be there—and I met the old boy himself. I told him what I wanted to see you about and he was nice enough to tell me why you should listen. Catch?"

I shook my head, trying to clear it. It had all looked so good, so possible, and now they were crowding me close.

"Yeah, I get it," I said. "The rats are gnawing on my door."

She laughed and I had an urge to rattle her teeth with five hard knuckles. But I didn't. I had no reason to hate her. We'd been playing a fast and dirty game, the both of us, and now the end had come for one of us.

"So you think you'll get it that easy," I said.

"I know I will."

"You know wrong, baby. It won't work."

"I hope you know what you're doing, Johnny. If you don't have that money to him by tomorrow morning he's turning it over to the insurance department."

"Stop scaring me," I said.

"And that'll mean the bonding company, Johnny. They'll toss you in jail."

Something else was in her eyes now besides the touch of victory. There was the shadow of a lonesome, inward fear that crept up into the blue.

"So what?" I demanded harshly. "They throw me in the can and I sit it out for a while. I don't know, maybe I've got it coming. I'm fed up with this racket, anyway I should have stuck to a dumb job."

"I'm offering you a way out, Johnny."

"The door's pretty narrow," I told her. "I'll get it slammed on my neck."

"You can't do anything else."

"Oh, now, can't I? Hell, baby, I can go to jail, just like I said, and have myself a little rest for a couple of weeks. It won't take long for the renewals to build up enough to pay off a lot more than seventy-five hundred."

"You'll lose your license."

"I was going to go into farming anyhow," I said. "Or something else. It doesn't make any difference." I knew I had her solid.

"And I'll watch you go broke," I said. "Cripes, baby, you'll be out of business before I am. I'd like that. I'd like it fine."

"I'll give you seventy-five hundred," she said, not looking at me.

"That's a long ways from twenty."

"I couldn't do it, Johnny. Honest!"

"That's tough."

"Mr. Greene—he's the man waiting out there—Mr. Greene said he'd go up to—"

"How much?"

"Eight," she said. "He hasn't got any more than that."

Before she could stop me I was out of the office and in front shaking hands with Mr. Greene.

"You going in this with Miss Noxon?"

His hand was like a piece of inner tube and his eyes were small and dumb.

"Yes, that's right."

"And how much do you figure on paying?"

"Well." He licked his lips with his tongue. "Well, she said she might get it for ten. I don't know much about these things, but—"

"Thanks," I told him. "And lots of luck."

I walked back to the office, wondering how long it'd take her to finish him off.

I went in and closed the door. She was sitting on the edge of the desk, swinging her legs back and forth, smiling at me.

"You just robbed me of two thousand bucks," she said. "That ought to make you happy."

"Yeah."

"He told you ten?"

"He told me ten."

"All right," she said, getting down. "I'll buy."

The rest of it didn't take very long. We drove down to a lawyer's, the same one I'd talked to about the divorce, and he drew up a bill of sale. Greene didn't have much to say but she insisted that I agree not to continue in the insurance business within a radius of two hundred miles. That part was okay with me and we stuck it in. After that we signed the original and some duplicates. She got the original and I stuck one of the carbons in my pocket along with the five thousand in cash and a certified check for another five which Greene had come up with. That Greene turned out to be a pretty regular guy. He even paid the lawyer.

I left them at the corner and walked back toward the office. I got a charge out of that clause she wanted put in the bill of sale. I had an extra list of all my clients and their addresses. If I wanted I could wander out west some place and set up shop. I had all these names and I could move right in on her again through the mails. I laughed and walked along faster.

That dumb dame didn't know what it was all about.

CHAPTER XIV

True Love

THE NEXT MORNING I checked out of my hotel room, tossed the luggage in the trunk of the Ford, and stopped at a diner just outside Waymart for breakfast.

I wasn't in any hurry.

I had some eggs, kidded around with the waitress for about an hour, and left her a dollar tip.

The road was icy, so I drove slow, not taking any chances. I wondered if I'd be driving back the same way. I guessed that I wouldn't.

Once in a while a guy gets tired of what he's been doing and, if he gets a break, he can sit down and think it over. Like I was doing. Thinking. And feeling lucky.

Hell, I could have wound up in the can—or made a young fortune. It was quite as simple as that. Only, somehow, it didn't seem to make much difference. It was done. Finished.

There was a place out west where a guy could go into the insurance business on a three cent stamp. There were farms up in the Catskills where a fellow could knock his brains out for the rest of his life and still not see the light of day. There were other things, too. Big things and little things. Good things and bad things. It was only a matter of choice.

I wondered, idly, if I ought to stop around and see the folks. Or, maybe, I could send them a check and write a short note. I was pretty sure they wouldn't give a damn as long as they got some money.

And Julie? When you go away you say good-bye to the girl, don't you? You call her a darling, or a whore, or whatever the case may be. You kiss her or you slap her silly and they both may mean the same thing. You're telling her that you love her. But when you don't feel much like doing either one of those things you ought to stay away. Right then I wasn't quite sure how it stood with me.

And your wife. You either live with her or you don't. If you're living together you just try to sneak away and hope that the blonde in the next room at the next hotel won't be too busy. But if you don't live with her you can save yourself plenty of time. You just jump on your feet and let the dust fly.

And the girl you sold your business to. You feel a little lousy about that but in a way you're glad. She's got plenty of problems figuring all the time how to strangle the person in front. You don't wish her any hard luck but you know that some day she'll wake up with a truckload of grief. And she's welcome. She can have it all for herself.

There's the help, too—the people who worked for you and lied for you. You tell yourself to forget about them, but you don't. You get yourself some checks and you sit up until three in the morning making them out. It's strange that you feel so much better after they've been mailed.

The next morning you get ready to clear the rest of the wreckage away. If you owe anybody any money you stop around and make a big shot out of yourself by giving it to them. Or you confirm the fact that you might be a heel and stay away. But it doesn't bother you any. It's the end of it—or the beginning. You never know until it's all clear and straight. Then, and only then, do you make your choice.

I drove down out of the hill country and onto the flats. The sun was up high and bright and the slush on the road slapped dully against the fenders. Ahead, the smoke from the tannery bored up into the sky and the tops of the buildings looked like gray bubbles stretched out on a white sheet.

I entered town, hit the lights just right and didn't have to stop until I reached the office.

I was through the door before I saw her. She tried to turn away, to retreat, but the elevator was on its way up again and she had no place to go.

"Hello, you bitch," I said.

There was nobody else in there and I pushed up against her, hard, slamming her into the wall. She winced and her eyes looked big and frightened.

"Where you going, Janet?"

"Please, Johnny."

"Little tramp," I breathed. "Stinking little tramp. What have you been up to now, baby?"

"Nothing." She kicked me once in the shins, but I got my knee in there and she couldn't do it again. "Please let me go, Johnny."

"Where's my money?"

"I won't tell you."

"That's great," I said. "You should've told me at the start that you were going to charge me over six thousand bucks for it. Only we wouldn't have done business, kid. I can get the same thing any place else for five."

"Oh, for God sakes, Johnny!"

"I want my coat back. You ran off with that, too. You can't wear that, baby."

She nodded and bit her lip.

"You'll get your damn coat," she said.

The outside door rattled and opened. An old woman in some rags came in and stared at us.

"Okay," I said to Janet. "Hit the road."

She went out like she'd heard me.

The old lady didn't know how to work the elevator so she rode along. I told her how it had been with me, the first time, going down into the basement and she got a big jolt out of that.

"I should have stayed there," I told her.

We got off and my passenger started yelling about a policy she wanted to turn in.

"Well, huckleberry!" I said to the glasses and the teeth that looked at me.

"Hello, Mr. Reagan."

"Yeah," I said. "So they got you back?"

"Mr. Connors wanted somebody steady," Miss Fisher told me stiffly.

"I don't know what I'm yacking about," I said. "He's the guy that's stuck."

"Always fresh, aren't you?"

"Sure. The old b—the old boy around?"

"I'll tell him you're here."

"Look," I said. "In five minutes I'm going to do a disappearing act. You might tell him that, too. I haven't got all day."

She trucked off, her snoot up in the air, and went around to his office.

The five minutes had almost run out when Moss Collins came over to me.

"Mr. Connors will see you now."

"How are you doing, Moss?"

He shrugged.

"We're flying straight again, Johnny."

I didn't say anything. Straight or crooked, I didn't give a damn how they were doing it.

"You made quite a rumble," he said. "Until it petered out."

"Yeah."

"I don't feel sore at you, Johnny—for firing me, that is."

"I don't care whether you are or not."

He pushed the door open and I went on inside. Connors sat behind his desk chewing a big cigar.

"Good morning," he said.

"I made it."

"I see that you did."

I yanked out twenty-five hundred bucks, added it to the certified check which I'd already endorsed, and dropped it in a pile in front of him.

"Count it," I said.

He did.

"It's all there, Johnny."

"He even gets a bonus," I said. "I already sent him a hundred bucks but he can have it for the wear and tear on his nerves. Now, give me a receipt."

He made out an official one and I stuffed it in my wallet.

"I didn't think you'd get it," he said.

"Well, you're not alone."

"Who did you swindle this time?"

"Nobody."

"That's difficult to believe."

"I sold out," I told him, getting a little sore. "You had my backside on a thistle bush and I had to get off. What more do you want?"

"Nothing, I guess." He tried to light the cigar but it was too wet, so he threw it away. "What plans have you got, Johnny?"

"I don't think that's any of your business."

"I'm still your father-in-law."

"Don't let it keep you awake," I said. "I won't tell anybody."

"I've sent Beverly to Las Vegas," he said. "You won't fight anything, will you?"

I'd wanted her out of my life and now that she was going I felt a small hollow inside my belly. There'd never been anything for us, never could be, and maybe that's the reason it seemed so unreal and stupid.

"No," I said. "I won't mess it up."

"That's good. I'd worried about that some."

If I'd never liked him before I started doing it right then. He was a good man, a plain man—simple, honest, direct. He was worrying about me giving him a hard time about something like that, when all along he could have had me sacked and thrown in the Bastille.

"No," I repeated, "there won't be any trouble. None at all."

"It's too bad it didn't work out, Johnny."

"Those things happen."

"We make them happen," he said quietly. "Don't ever mistake that."

"Sure."

"You don't know what you cost yourself, Johnny. I had plans for you, Johnny—big ones. When I got back I was going to take you in as a partner, build you folks a real house, do a hell of a lot of big things for you."

No one had ever given me anything except a slap in the mouth when I was a kid. And I didn't want anything from him. Nothing.

"I guess I'll shove off," I said.

"Try to play it straight, Johnny."

"Yeah."

"You haven't done anything so awful wrong," he said, leaning back in his chair. "A lot of people would say that what you did was dishonest. I don't know. Sometimes folks learn by doing things wrong and they make sure that it doesn't happen again. That's what counts."

I edged off toward the door.

"Okay," I said.

"There's one other thing you ought to know, Johnny."

"What's that?"

He got up and shuffled around the desk.

"Perhaps I shouldn't tell you."

"Then, keep it to yourself," I said.

"Remember Janet—the little girl who introduced us?"

I pushed the door closed again.

"Drop it," I told him. "I don't want to hear anything about her."

"She's in love with you," he said. "Deeply in love."

"Yeah?"

"She was just up here." He fumbled around and found another cigar. He looked straight at me while he was lighting it. "I gave her sixty-four hundred dollars of your money, Johnny."

"What!"

"Well, I say it was yours. Maybe it was and maybe it wasn't. A couple of days after you and Beverly were married I got a long cable from her. Said she had some money that belonged to me. I couldn't make head nor tail to it so I had my attorney look her up. She finally told the whole story, how she was in love with you and that she was afraid you'd be short in your accounts."

"She made me short enough," I said, remembering that day at the bank.

"Not here, Johnny. When the auditor got finished with the books he found some irregularities but he also found a sixty-four hundred dollar surplus. That's the money she turned over to me. And that's the money I just gave back to her."

"Hot damn!"

"She's in love with you," Connors told me again. "I asked her to come up here but when I offered her the money she didn't want it. She told me how you'd been overdrawn at the bank that day—she had misjudged the account, Johnny—and she felt sick about it. She wouldn't tell me why she just didn't go down and redeposit it the day you had the trouble."

I remembered how I'd slapped her around the office, cursing her and the way she'd ran out wearing my overcoat.

"Women are nuts," I said.

He shrugged and returned to his desk.

"She may have done you harm, Johnny, but I'm sure she meant only good," he said. "You'll have to take it from there."

"How come you gave it to her?" I wanted to know. "Just now, I mean? What if I hadn't been able to raise the dough?"

"But I knew you would," he said, smiling. "I talked to Miss Noxon yesterday afternoon. I could see nothing but success in her venture. You needed money and she needed your business."

"It didn't have to happen," I said, growing cold all over. "I shucked it out for peanuts and all the time I could have sailed through it, easy."

"You're out of it, Johnny. That's worth something."

"Yeah. It's worth about twenty grand that I'm out of."

"Ten years from now you'll never know."

"Who's kidding who?" I asked. "Twenty-four hours after I'm dead I'll still be seeing all that money!"

"You'll get over it."

"Like a broken back."

"In case you want to see the girl," he said, "she's working out of town at a motel. Shady Lawn. Know where it is?"

"On the old Lime Road."

He nodded and sucked on the cigar.

"Couple of old folks own it. The girl says they want to sell and she seems mighty interested in it. The new highway's going through there, you know, and it'll be a real hot spot. You might stop over there and see her."

"I'll see her in hell," I said.

He kept talking about the motel, the money that could be made and the steady life it would be, until I got sick of it. After he'd repeated the same things three times I told him good-bye and jumped out of the door.

I went down to the street, got in the car and pointed it in the direction of Route 6, the main road west. I flipped the radio switch and got an earful of "Turkey in the Straw" and nineteen different reasons why I should buy a Family Protective insurance policy. I decided that Cynthia Noxon wouldn't like it one bit when I started bleeding her customers through the mails.

All I had to do was get out there and buy myself a bunch of stamps.

I drove real close to the restaurant where Julie Wilson worked. I didn't even slow the car.

I didn't think of anybody, really, except Janet and the screwy things she'd done. How the hell can a woman love a man and still throw him to the cannibals?

I was almost to the city line when I noticed the envelope on the floor. Even before I picked it up and opened it I knew what was in there. Sixty-four hundred bucks. No note. Just the money. Money with perfume on it.

When I got to the intersection I was knocking off fifty. I didn't have to slow up. Route 6 was sharp left but old Lime Road was straight ahead and the light was green.

Shady Lawn, he'd said. A motel. Cripes, that was a deadfall if I'd ever heard of one. A guy could work his legs off to the knees on a deal like that. People coming all hours of the nights and knocking holes in the walls and getting sick like dogs. People swiping your towels and bending the keys when they used them for bottle openers. People keeping you so busy you didn't have much time for anything else.

I slowed, thinking about Janet and how she was going to start yelling when I walked in. I grinned and kicked the gas pedal on the Ford. She could only yell just so long and I could sit that out. Then I'd tell her. All of it. The way it had been and the way it could be. Later, after we'd talked it out, we could do something else. Something real personal.

Like holding hands.

Or something else you haven't read about in this book.

The End

About the Author

Prince of the Pulps, Orrie Edwin Hitt, was a franchise unto himself. He did not complete his first novel until he was almost forty and wrote his last a mere fourteen years later, in 1968, but in between he racked up an impressive catalog, mostly paperback originals, classic pulps from the 50s and 60s, detailing the seedier side of life, the poor, wanton, or depraved. Hitt wrote about desperate people—men and women—people in need who would do things that most of us would never dare. And yet, somehow, his characters were precisely those people that you couldn't get enough of and couldn't help but root for.

A lifelong resident of Upstate New York, Orrie Hitt died at the age of fifty-nine, on December 7, 1975. He left a wife and four children. And a legacy of memorable books and characters that will be read and remembered for a long time to come, for not only their style and mood but for what they say about the human condition.

Also on Blackbird . . .

Check out our other great titles at:

BLACKBIRD BOOKS
www.bbirdbooks.com